DESTINED
to Love Again

LOIS CURRAN

Paperback-Press
an imprint of A & S Publishing
A & S Holmes, Inc.

ISBN: 1-945669-09-8
ISBN-13: 978-1-945669-09-5

DEDICATION
To my three sons: Kenny, Lon & Jason Waterman.

ACKNOWLEDGMENTS

First of all I'd like to thank God for everything He's done for me.

A special thanks to my incredible family who encourage and support me in my writing dreams. I love all of you so much.

To my work friends who stood behind me and walked with me through this endeavor, I appreciate all you do for me. You guys are the best.

Roxan Gregory, thank you for the crash course in horses so I could accurately describe riding lessons on paper. Any mistakes in the stable scenes are mine.

Thanks to my good friend and Author Susan Keene who critiqued my manuscript and taught me a lot along the way.

And last but not least, a special thank you to my publisher, Sharon Kizziah-Holmes. Thank you for believing in me.

CHAPTER ONE

No doubt about it, she would be okay…

The early morning sun danced through palm trees and cast shadows on the two-story red brick structure that stretched nearly a block. Abby Dennison stopped at the bottom of the cobblestone steps and looked at Brighton Hall.

A warm moist breeze drifted inland from the bay. It lifted her hair and tickled the back of her neck as she climbed the boarding school steps. She smiled and pulled in a long breath. Coming to Brighton was the right decision.

She hesitated at the arched entryway, straightened her shoulders, turned the knob, pushed the door open, and stepped inside. A middle-aged woman gave a cursory nod as she clip-clopped across the sandstone tile corridor in sensible, low-heeled pumps. "Good morning." She stopped, tucked a strand of dark hair behind her ear, and eyed Abby. A spark of recognition lit her eyes. "You're the new nurse. I'm Carolyn Pringle, the assistant dean of students. We met at your interview."

"Oh. Yes, I remember." Abby remembered her face, and the over-powering cologne that irritated her nose.

"You're early." She turned her wrist to look at her watch.

Abby nodded. "A little, I like to get situated before my day starts."

"Well, let me know if you need anything." She turned to walk away. "Oh, and welcome to Brighton Academy."

As she made her way down the hallway, a smile tugged at the corners of her mouth. Thirty-five wasn't too old to start over and she was ready for a new beginning.

She turned the key in the lock, pushed the door open and walked in. She stopped and stepped back. A man with his back to her rummaged through the supply closet. "What are you doing in here?"

The intruder whirled around and banged his head on the open cabinet door. "Don't scream. I belong here. I'm Sam, from maintenance." He held up a bandaged hand. "I hurt myself."

Abby stared at him as his words sunk in.

"I've got a key, see?" The man held up a key ring. "I was just getting a bandage."

She laid a hand on her chest. "You scared the daylights out of me." Her heartbeat slowed somewhat, the taste of her fear subsided. "I'm the new nurse. Abby."

"I'm sorry I scared you." His gaze shifted to the tape, gauze, and antiseptic packets he'd lifted from the supply cabinet. "Is it okay if I take these?" He motioned to his other hand that clutched the stock and took a few steps toward her. The pungent scent of Betadine and rubbing alcohol stung her nose.

She sighed. "Sure, go ahead."

"I'll get out of your way." He edged toward the door and slipped into the hall.

She stood in the doorway and leaned her back against the jamb. Arms crossed over her chest, she watched the back of the tall man with dark wavy hair and broad shoulders saunter down the hall.

* * *

Abby's first client, a 16 year-old girl who complained of menstrual cramps, tapped her toes and stood with her hands on her hips. "Can you please just give me some Midol? I'm gonna be late for class."

"First things first. Do you have any allergies?" Abby flipped through the girl's chart, noting the "NKA"—no known allergies.

"No allergies. Sheesh, all I'm asking for is a lousy Midol not the third degree."

"Fine." Abby rolled her eyes. She dispensed the tablets. Little miss impatience swallowed them in one gulp, tossed the paper cup in the trash and scurried out the door, without so much as a thank you.

That was an easy fix, Abby thought. She hummed to herself. Her move to Tampa was the right decision, she could feel it. Yes, life looked good at this moment. It beat life in Orlando where every day reminded her of Robert.

A year ago she broke up with the man she loved and trusted. It didn't seem possible, a seven year relationship gone in an instant. Would the memory of him ever fade? The past needed to stay in the past. God restored her life and showed her she didn't belong in a live-in relationship without the sanctity of a wedding ring.

A knock on the door brought her back to the present. She turned as the maintenance man stepped back inside.

She smiled. "Did you forget something?"

"These bandages keep slipping off. Can I get something that will stay on better?"

"Let me see." She reached for his hands. His left hand wasn't bad, but the right one had a couple of weepy blisters. Other than the abrasions, his hands were smooth, not at all what one would expect of a laborer. "What in the world did you do?"

"I waxed and buffed the halls in dormitory two on Friday." He looked almost apologetic as he peered down at his sore hand.

"Don't you wear gloves?" Abby guided him to the infirmary.

"I forgot them." He shook his head. "I've got to do better."

"Yeah, I'd say so. Are you new here?"

"Been here about six months, since November."

"Have a seat." Abby pointed to the exam table and Sam obediently stepped up on the pullout rung and plopped down. She stepped to the supply cabinet, opened the double doors and checked the contents.

"Sorry about this morning. I don't usually help myself without asking. I wasn't aware you'd be here today."

"No harm done. Don't worry about it." Abby turned her head and smiled at him. She found what she needed, put it on a cart and took it to where he sat.

Sam shifted positions and extended his hand toward Abby. "If I'd known you were starting this morning, I wouldn't have barged in."

"Actually I'm here a week early. I wasn't scheduled to start until next Monday but I finished things up sooner than I'd planned." She pulled on latex gloves, opened the bottle of hydrogen peroxide and saturated a large cotton ball. "So I called Dean Williams last week. He said he could use me now."

Sam nodded. "I'm sure he could. Katie, the last nurse left three weeks ago and it's been a little crazy around here. Mrs. Pringle arranged a substitute for a couple hours each afternoon, but that didn't work out well."

"No, I don't imagine. Kids can't line up their ailments with a scheduled time frame. Well, I'm here now so hopefully things will be better." She dabbed Sam's palm with the wet cotton ball. "This will feel a little cool but it shouldn't sting." She squeezed the medicine onto his blister and when he didn't flinch, she looked up at him. A pair of the most intense blue eyes she had ever seen stared back at her. The heat crept up her neck. "When was the last time you had a tetanus booster?"

"A few months ago."

"You're okay then." Abby pushed the lever on the trash can with her foot and tossed in the cotton ball.

She had him wave his hand around to dry the medicine so the bandage would stick. "There. That'll help. Don't forget those gloves next time."

"Yes ma'am." He saluted her and smiled for the first time, revealing white, straight teeth. He had a nice smile, very nice smile.

Abby grinned too, but suddenly her throat felt dry and she was at a loss for words.

Sam scooted from the exam table. "How about I show you around the grounds during lunch? You know, to pay you back for taking care of my hand."

Abby looked at him, and made a quick decision. "I would love it."

"See you at noon then," he said as he turned and walked away.

She watched him go and reminded herself not to read more into his invitation than he intended. "Come on Abby," she chided herself. "Keep it simple."

* * *

As Sam Ford walked away from the new nurse, he raked his fingers through his hair and did his best not to whistle. He'd heard a new nurse was coming to Brighton but he wasn't prepared for one that looked and smelled as good as Abby.

He replayed their last encounter as he walked down the hall. He could have taken care of his own hand, but her touch was light, gentle, and perfect.

Deep in thought about her slender hands, smooth wrists, he nearly collided with one of the students.

The boy grabbed his arm and shot him a dirty look. "Watch it, dude." His eyes widened. "Oh, sorry, Mr. Ford."

"Don't worry about it." Sam gave the kid a good-natured shrug and shook his head. "I wasn't watching where I was going. See you around."

The boy grinned at him and went on his way.

Sam continued down the corridor. When he opened the door and walked in the utility closet, he groaned a little. All of the school's supplies that were delivered on Friday still needed to be unpacked and put away. He grabbed a utility knife from the shelf and cut open one of the cardboard boxes.

"Hey, Sam." His supervisor's voice crackled over the walkie-talkie he wore on his belt.

He unhooked the two-way, and answered with a "Yeah."

"Grab your mop and head to the kitchen. Florence has made another mess. Somehow she managed to knock the water cooler off its stand."

"I'm on it." Sam slipped the devise back on his belt and then rounded up his gear.

He saw Sara as he wheeled the mop bucket down the hall, and for the thousandth time since November, he marveled at how much love and pride filled his heart when he saw his daughter. But when the fourteen-year-old saw him, her violet eyes gazed downward and she slid a hand through her brunette hair.

Sam stopped and leaned on the mop handle.

"How's it going?"

"I'm cool." Her eyes darted up and down the hall. Sam knew she would be horrified if anyone suspected her dad was the janitor, but the hall was deserted. "I've got this major test in Algebra today and I'm really nervous. Gotta nail it."

"You'll do great."

"Whatever." She shrugged and relaxed a little.

Sam saw nosey Mrs. Pringle turn the corner and head in their direction. He knew the conversation was over.

"Gotta go. Bye Da…Mr. Ford," Sara said and fled down the hall.

Sam watched his daughter hustle away and wondered if he'd made a mistake coming to Brighton. She was horrified when he took the job to be near her. So horrified in fact, that he agreed not to reveal his identity to anyone here. At the time, it seemed like the fatherly thing to do.

Sara was humiliated at the slightest hint her friends might learn she was the daughter of the maintenance man. Since her materialistic mother raised her, Sam didn't blame his daughter for feeling the way she did. But understanding didn't take away the pain that stabbed at his heart every time she shunned him. He longed for a normal relationship.

Patience, he thought, it'll come. Too much time was already wasted, now he intended to bond with her. He was going to be a real father, take care of her, protect her, and most of all show her how much he loved her.

Sam shoved all thoughts aside as he stepped into

the kitchen and saw the puddle of water on the floor, and the water cooler lying empty on its side.

Florence Decker, Brighton's head cook, was on her knees with a towel in an attempt to clean up her mess. Her gray hair was askew. She looked up, pressed her lips together and swiped the beads of sweat off her forehead.

"Again?" Sam asked. He took her arm and helped her stand.

"I'm sorry, Sam. I had a stack of trays up to here." She held her hand chin high. "I ran smack dab into the cooler. I'm such a klutz."

"Yes, but a sweet one." He looked her up and down. "You should have the nurse check you out, make sure you're not hurt."

"The nurse is here?"

"Yep."

Florence shook her head. "Oh, I'm fine. I didn't even drop the trays, just did a number on that cooler." She paused and adjusted her hairnet. "I'm sorry I had to bother you again. I know how busy you are."

"Hey, life around here would be boring if I wasn't at your beck-and-call." Sam pushed his mop back and forth, and then transferred it to the bucket wringer. "I'd never get to see you if you weren't accident prone." He winked at her. Florence had mothered him since the day he arrived and he had grown fond of the elderly lady. "You keep me on my toes."

Florence smiled, and patted him on the shoulder. "You're a good man, Sam Ford."

He cleaned up the mess, washed his hands in the

sink taking care not to ruin the bandage Abby put on it earlier in the day. Florence handed him a freshly baked cinnamon roll. It dripped with gooey icing. The aroma of yeast was so sharp his mouth watered.

"You're bound and determined to make me fat," he said, taking a man-sized bite of the roll.

"A few extra pounds wouldn't hurt you a bit." She handed him a mug of steaming coffee. "Can you stay for a minute while I peel some vegetables?"

"For a minute." Sam licked the remaining icing from the corners of his mouth. From his perch on a stool nearby, he watched Florence's swift movements. She peeled potatoes and carrots at lightning speed. He was mesmerized as he watched the scraps mound up in the bottom of the sink. He enjoyed the comfortable repartee they shared. With her potatoes peeled and soaking, she pulled a stool up and sat across from Sam. She drew her brows together and pursed her lips into a frown. "What happened to your hand?"

"Oh, nothing serious. Just some blisters, too much buffing Friday." He looked down at his hand and remembered Abby's gentle touch.

"Let me guess, you weren't wearing gloves?"

"Forgot 'em."

"My word, Son, you need someone to look after you. Don't you know you have to wear gloves when you're manhandling that buffer?"

"I got the same lecture from the new nurse this morning."

"So you've met her? What's she like?"

He shrugged. "Nice, I guess."

"I hated to see Katie go. She was the best nurse we've had in a long time. Is she as nice as Katie?"

"I barely spoke to her. Too early to tell."

"Good looking?"

"Sorta."

"Well, come on. Fill me in. What does she look like?"

"She's tall, blondish hair and green eyes, I think."

"What do you mean, you think? Either they're green or they're not. Which is it?"

Sam scowled. "Yeah, they're green."

"Is she single?"

Her young friend smiled. He knew what she had on her mind. "Put your bow and arrow away, Cupid."

"You didn't answer. Is she single?"

"I think so."

"That means you know so." Laughter gushed from the lovable old matchmaker. "You're already impressed with her, aren't you? Come on Sam, you might as well own up to it."

"You're just too much, you know that?" Sam gave her hand a squeeze, then scooted his stool back, took the last swig of coffee and wiped his mouth with the back of his hand. "I've got work to do. See you later."

He left the kitchen and spent the next two hours stacking supplies on the shelves in the utility closet. Finished with that procrastinated job, he gathered his equipment and made his way to the academic section.

He swept a pile of dirt into the dustpan and dumped it into the trash bin. He looked up and saw Sara push the door to the library open and enter. She passed right by him, yet didn't speak. He sighed. When he moved to Tampa six months ago he was excited about becoming a part of his daughter's life. He'd envisioned spending a lot of weekends with her, but it hadn't worked out that way. He was lucky if he had a Sunday afternoon with his daughter once a month. The secrecy prevented them from doing anything together except to visit at his apartment and that wasn't exciting for a teenager.

The secrecy ate at him all the time.

When he made the promise to Sara he didn't consider the consequences of his decision. Circumstances were different now. He became a Christian and the lie tugged at his heart. Worse yet, he was teaching Sara a lack of integrity and he hated it.

The sound of the bell echoed in the hallway. Soon it would be time for lunch, with Abby. He smiled. Wouldn't Florence have a hay-day with that bit of news?

CHAPTER TWO

Abby finished her morning charting early. She glanced at the clock. Sam would be here in a few minutes. She walked across the office to the window and looked out. She could see the front of the campus. She ran her fingers over the pane and gazed out at the quiet grounds. Everything felt serene and slow-paced compared to the hustle bustle life at Orlando General.

She sensed, rather than heard, someone behind her. She turned and saw Sam standing in the open doorway.

"Ready?" he asked.

Abby grabbed her keys and wallet from her purse and slipped them in her pocket. "Ready," she said and followed Sam across the threshold.

She pulled the office door closed behind her and made sure it locked. Sam's aftershave, something woodsy and tantalizing, wafted over her making her heart give a little flutter.

"I thought we could get something to go in the

deli and head to the park, if that's okay with you."

"Sounds perfect."

Abby walked beside Sam down the wide Victorian corridor, past the cafeteria to a small alcove that housed the *Brighton Deli.* She noticed a sign that told her low fat turkey and romaine was the special. "No salad for me today. I'm starved."

"Nice to see a woman who actually eats." Sam shot her a smile.

"Yeah, I have an unbelievable metabolism. Drives my sister crazy."

He smiled. "How many siblings do you have?"

"Two sisters. How about you?"

"Just an older brother, Ken."

Sam pressed his palm on the middle of her back. His hand was warm and assertive without being pushy. "Corn dogs okay with you?"

She nodded. "Sounds great."

He stepped up to the counter. "Two corn dogs, two large fries with extra catsup, and two sweet teas," he said to the redheaded, all-smiles girl, who appeared more than happy to be taking his order. She had the food and drinks bagged and placed on the ledge by the time he paid the cashier.

A gentle breeze, warm and fragrant with the smell of orange blossoms, played with Abby's hair as soon as she walked through the glass doors at the rear exit and stepped outside. Beside her, Sam, arms loaded with paper bags, guided her to a golf cart parked at the curb.

"Hop in." He deposited the bags in the back and slid behind the wheel. "This is my transportation around the grounds."

Seated next to him, she let her eyes drift toward the flowers that lined the walkways, the bright colors erupted in the sunlight. The powdery blue sky was bright and dotted with white, wispy clouds that lolled along the horizon and drifted overhead. She inhaled the scent of newly mown grass as they rolled past the swimming pool and turned a sharp left into the academy's private park.

He set the bag of food on an empty picnic table and spread the napkins out while she unpacked the food. He waited for Abby to scoot onto the bench, and then sat across from her.

"So, how's your first day going so far?" He dipped the end of a corn dog into a dollop of mustard and took a bite.

"Good. I think I'm going to like it here," Abby said, thinking about her life here and the one she left behind, where the one man she trusted let her down. He wouldn't stand beside her when she needed him. She had no one to blame but herself. *When you compromise with the world, your heart turns away from God and you get yourself in a mess.*

"It's a pretty laid back place." Sam interrupted her thoughts. He took a swig of his tea. "And lots to do here. Did anyone tell you about the perks we get?"

"Uh huh." Abby wrestled with her corn dog. She wasn't as hungry as she thought. Her eyes were always bigger than her stomach. "I'm excited about the riding stable. I've always wanted to learn to ride. Do they offer lessons?"

"Not for staff, but I can teach you." He dipped a

fry into the catsup and popped it into his mouth.

She swallowed her bite and took a sip of tea. "You ride?"

He nodded. "Yeah. I grew up around horses. Started riding when I was a kid. I haven't had time to do much of it since I graduated college, but got back in to it when I took this job." He winked. "You'd be in good hands."

Abby stared at him. Why was a college graduate working as a maintenance man?

"I might just take you up on that," she said.

They shared easy banter as they nibbled away at their lunch and enjoyed the warm breeze that drifted inland from the gulf. Abby finished her last French fry and slid the wrapper into the bag.

Sam crumpled his trash, took hers, and threw it in the bin. "Come on." He nudged her toward the cart. "I'll show you the stables."

"Oh, look." Abby stopped and pointed to a huge, oak tree with a bunch of names carved in the trunk. "It says, 'David was here—1961'. Wow, that's a long time ago."

"Yeah. That was back when Brighton was an orphanage."

She slid into the passenger seat. "Hmm. Why'd it become a school?"

Sam turned the key and the cart jumped to life. "The state pulled funding and the orphanage had to close." He slowed the vehicle as he approached a narrow trail. The sound of the tires changed as the cart moved from blacktop to gravel and crackled under its weight.

"I like the old-world flair that's still here."

Sam nodded. "The school's been around a long time but it hasn't lost its New England feel."

"Yeah, it's like being at Yale…with humidity." She laughed.

"You've got that right." He chuckled, the sound of his voice, deep and rich, was pleasant.

She looked at the man seated next to her and took a deep breath. She liked to ride in the cart, her hair blowing in the wind, as she listened to his vivid description of the locality.

Sam pulled over and shut the engine off. The aroma of hay and horses, blended together, drifted up Abby's nose. Several of the animals ran free in the field. One sleek mare pranced behind a man who led her by a rope toward the round pen used to train the animals.

"Hey, Fred, how's it going?" Sam called out to the man.

"Not bad." Fred stopped and patted the horse's neck. The horse turned toward him and nuzzled his palm.

The animal was enormous, with a reddish brown coat that glistened in the noonday sun.

"Nice day for training," Sam said.

"Sure is." The caretaker plucked off his baseball cap and fanned himself. "If you're here for a ride, help yourself. The tack room's unlocked."

"No, we're just here to look today." Sam navigated Abby to the fenced paddock where four horses moseyed about.

She hooked her arms over the top railing of the fence and watched the horses. She had a respectful fear of them, yet they intrigued her. She loved them from afar. They were so big and intimidating. She glanced toward Sam, who was smiling.

"What?" she asked.

"You," he said. "You look like a kid on Christmas morning, all wide-eyed and excited."

Warmth rushed up her neck. "They're beautiful."

"Yes, they are, smart too. When a steed is old enough to train, Fred lets me help. I'm amazed at how fast they respond to gentle instruction. You know, people could learn a thing or two from horses."

Abby glanced at Sam. There was something about the tender inflection in his voice when he talked about the animals that told her this was a man she could trust, and not just with horses.

"If you're not doing anything Saturday, I could give you your first lesson." He leaned on the fence, and twiddled a blade of grass.

She looked at the massive build of the horses, and her stomach turned over, and did a couple of flip-flops. "I don't know…"

"You don't have to do anything you're not ready for; just remember, all the horses here are gentle. We'll take it nice and slow until you get used to being around the horse. I won't put you on one until you are comfortable."

"Okay." She inhaled deeply and released a slow breath. "I guess I'm as ready as I'll ever be."

"I'll meet you here on Saturday then. Is ten okay?"

"Ten it is."

He looked at his watch. "We better head back."

She nodded and walked with him to the golf cart

and slid into the passenger seat.

Sam turned the vehicle toward the visitor's entrance and took her back a different way than they came, past the baseball field and the gym.

"There's a small lake on the other side of those trees." Sam pointed to a grove of oaks. "If we had time, I'd swing by and show you. It's a great place to kick back and relax. Sometimes I take out one of the canoes."

"Sounds peaceful."

"It is, believe me."

"The entire campus has an aura of tranquility." She marveled at the colorful flowerbeds that emanated the heady perfumes of spring. The palm and oak trees swayed in the breeze. She spotted a white crane as he sauntered around a bush, no doubt looking for a lizard for his lunch.

Sam pulled the cart next to the curb and dropped her off at the main entrance.

"Thanks for the guided tour," she said.

"My pleasure. I'll see you later." He gave her a two finger wave as he sped off.

When Abby approached her office, she saw her sister Emily plopped cross-legged on the floor, her back propped against the wall, and her nose buried in a magazine.

"What are you doing here?" Abby unlocked the door. "Why aren't you at work?"

"The air conditioning went out this morning and Doc cancelled today's appointments." Emily shrugged her shoulders. "So, I have the rest of the day off."

"That's great."

"So, where have you been?" Emily rose from her cross-legged position and smoothed her Capris.

"Lunch in the park. Then a tour of the grounds."

"By yourself?"

"No. With Sam. He's one of the guys who works here."

"Interesting." Emily's eyebrows bounced up and down.

"Don't get the wrong idea. I just met him." Abby opened the door and ushered her sister inside. "So, what brings you here?"

"I came to have lunch with you."

"You could have called."

"How was I to know you'd pick up a guy on your first day?"

Only Emily could razz her this way.

"I'm telling you, little sister, it was nothing."

"Oh no?" Emily threw her a sly wink.

Abby's eyebrows shot up. "Emily, you know good and well I am not interested in starting anything…with anyone." However she couldn't stop a slow grin. "But he is one good-looking man. You should see him."

"I'd like to. What's he look like?"

Abby's mind conjured up the handsome handyman. "Tall, at the minimum six inches taller than me. So that makes him at least 6'2". Let's see…dark wavy hair and the bluest eyes. Reminds me of Patrick Dempsey. Real buff, like he works out or something."

"Wow. He sounds gorgeous."

"He is. And the best thing, he's not full of himself, if you know what I mean. He seems like a really nice guy."

"Nice guy is good." Emily shot her a look.

"He only showed me around at lunch. No biggie."

"Whatever you say."

Abby slid into her desk chair and motioned for Emily to sit in the chair situated to the side. She opened her drawer, pulled out a breakfast bar and tossed it to her sister. "To hold you over until you can get a real lunch."

"Great. I brought something for you, too." Emily opened her purse; she fished out an oversized Snickers bar and slid it across the desk. "For your afternoon snack attack."

"Thanks."

Emily got up and wandered to the window. She tapped fingers on the pane and peered out. "I'm glad you're finally interested in someone other than Robert."

"I dated some in Orlando. You know that."

Emily turned, walked to Abby, leaned forward and rested her palms on the desk. "Yeah, but you weren't excited about anyone. Not the way you sound about this guy."

"Come on, Em. I'm not 'excited,'" she made air quotes, "about anyone."

"But you're over Robert, aren't you?"

Abby drew her brows together and eyed Emily. A tear formed in her eye. What was going on with her sister? Why did she bring up Robert today? "Yes, I'm over him. Hey, don't worry about me. I'm okay now. Really."

"I just want you to be happy." Emily took her

sister's hand and gave it a gentle squeeze. "You know I love you, don't you?"

Abby nodded. She stood and wrapped her arms around her sister. "I love you, too. Thanks for caring so much."

Abby's thoughts drifted to the long, lonely nights she endured after Robert refused to marry her. Sleep wouldn't come no matter how hard she willed it. She'd call Emily in the wee hours of the morning and somehow Emily would calm her broken heart just enough to get her through another day. She had always been there for her, always available to listen and offer a shoulder to lean on. How could she have made it through without her sister? Her sister, but also the best friend she ever had. Abby smiled.

* * *

A persistent ring of the phone woke Sam Tuesday morning. He rubbed his eyes and looked at the clock. As he shook the sleep-induced fog from his brain, he grabbed the receiver and muttered a hello.

"Hi Sam. It's me."

"Linda?" He sat up. Why was Sara's mother calling so early? "What's wrong? Is Sara alright?"

"She's fine. You sound sleepy. I didn't wake you did I?"

"What do you think?" Sam couldn't find his bedroom slippers, so he padded down the hall to the kitchen, barefoot. He flipped the switch on the coffee maker.

"Don't be so grouchy. I wanted to catch you

before you left for work."

"What's going on?" He pulled a mug from the cabinet.

"Well, I just wanted to let you know that Ben and I are going to move to Curacao in a month."

"Moving?" He set the cup down hard. "You can't just haul Sara away from me."

He'd changed his entire lifestyle so he could be close to his daughter. Now Linda thought she could just swoop in and take her away.

"Calm down, Sam. Sara won't go with us. I want her to stay at Brighton."

Sam balanced the phone between his ear and shoulder and used both hands to siphon some coffee from the unfinished pot. This would be strong but he didn't care. He needed the caffeine. "Let me get this straight. You're going to leave Sara here and move to an island?"

Linda had always been impulsive, but to move out of the country and leave her fourteen-year-old daughter to fend for herself didn't make sense, not even for Linda.

"Don't make it sound like I'm going to abandon her." Linda's tone was crisp and deliberate, like she sounded when she knew what she was about to do was wrong. "Ben has sold a good portion of his business and he's going to semi-retire. Curacao has been a dream of his for years."

"I see." It finally clicked in. Maybe he'd ingested enough caffeine to clear his mind. Good old Ben. Linda married him two years ago. Shortly thereafter Sara ended up in boarding school. Now he was anxious to whisk Linda away to an island.

"Sam..." Linda hesitated. He heard a catch in her voice. "You'll have to be in charge of Sara now. With Ben and me so far away we couldn't possibly take care of the day to day things that might come up."

"What does Sara think about this?"

"I haven't told her yet. I'll break the news to her this morning. But I'm sure she'll be okay with it. She just won't want you to blow your cover and have her friends find out you're her father. You know she hates it that you're the school janitor."

That cut Sam. "Then how do you propose I be in charge of her?"

"No problem. I'll take care of it. I'm going to make you her legal guardian. I'll get the appropriate paperwork turned into the school today after I talk to Sara. Then I'll set up an appointment for tomorrow for us all to meet with the assistant dean. No one at the school will ever have to know you're her father."

Sam sucked in a deep breath and willed his voice to stay calm. "No. No more lies."

"But..."

"Linda, I'm not going to add more lies to the already existing ones. I can't keep doing this. It's not right."

"You're not lying. You just haven't told anyone you're her father."

"Same thing."

He heard a harrumph from Linda. "Well I'll figure something out. But we need to get this taken care of as soon as possible."

"Set up the appointment with Mrs. Pringle and

I'll be there. Just remember, I'm not going to lie anymore."

"Whatever you say, Sam."

"I hope Sara will be okay with this." Sam massaged his brow and took another sip from his mug; the thick hot liquid soothed his throat. "She's so young to be separated from her mother."

"She'll adjust."

"Like she adjusted when she found out I was her father?"

"I know you blame me for keeping her from you. I probably should have told you as soon as I knew I was pregnant. But I kept putting it off. Then it just seemed too late to tell you. I don't know. I had a lot of things going on back then. I had to take care of myself, you know."

Renewed resentment boiled inside him. Even the thought of Linda's antics left a sour taste in his mouth. He'd heard all her lame excuses before, for almost three years. "I had the right to know you were pregnant. I would have been there for you, for both of you. It was cruel and selfish of you to keep her from me." He took the last swig of his coffee and set the mug in the sink. "Linda, I hate pretending I'm not her father."

"Now, that's not my fault. You're the one who chose to quit your job, move to Tampa, and take that janitor's job. You're a doctor, for pity's sake. You could have moved down here and taken a respectable position at the hospital."

Respectable, that's what it's all about with Linda. Position, status, and prestige were the only things she cared about. It was the reason he couldn't commit fifteen years ago.

"We've been through all that." He shook his head in disgust. He refused to argue with her. There were good reasons why he walked away from his heart-wrenching job at the hospital in Atlanta. He never doubted his decision. His only regret was not being honest about to Sara.

"Well you could have opened a private practice or something…"

Linda's nagging was beginning to grate on him. "You know as well as I do, small practices don't exist anymore."

"You can't blame the child for being embarrassed. Well not of you, per se, but what you do. What's she supposed to say to her friends? 'This is my dad the janitor who used to be a well-known physician.' Come on Sam, get real."

"I don't blame her for any of this. I blame you. You robbed me of twelve years of my daughter's life. I just want her to be happy."

"Oh, really? Well let me tell you, she was happy when she found out you were her father until you switched professions and decided to go blue collar. I'll never understand you, Sam. You spent all that time training to be a physician, and look at you now. A janitor, good grief, such a waste."

Sam sighed. It had taken him a year to land the job at Brighton. When he found the position at the boarding school, it seemed like the perfect answer. He'd be able to monitor his daughter and have a less hectic job at the same time. He hadn't counted on Sara's humiliation over his position as a janitor. But what did he know about teenagers? Thanks to

Linda, he never realized he was a father. He knew how to heal sick kids, but had no idea how to get it right with his own daughter.

"Sam, I'm going to have to go. Are you willing to take care of Sara or not?" Linda said in an unfriendly tone.

Of course he would. What an absurd question. But to Linda he only said, "Yes."

He hit the end button and laid the phone on the counter, turned on the water and cleaned the same granite top he cleaned before she called. How could Linda be so self-centered? What was wrong with her, or maybe it was what was wrong with him? Why had he postponed the inevitable—coming clean about his paternity? He glanced at the card stuck to the refrigerator—Michael Sullivan, Brighton Academy Chaplin—and thought about calling him. Too late, he was probably at early services by now.

He ran a hand through his tangled hair and headed for the shower. Hadn't he always tried to be open and up-front with people? Always, until he moved here. Now his life revolved around lies and deceit.

Since he gave his life to the Lord, his choice to go along with the duplicity ate away at him. The decision to keep a promise to his daughter or be honest about her, tore him up. How could he be a good father if, by example, he taught Sara it's okay to be deceptive?

He made a decision as he got dressed. He had to talk to Mike, the sooner the better.

CHAPTER THREE

Abby pushed her chair away from the desk, yawned, and stretched her arms high over her head. She checked the ninth grade charts and made sure everything was in order for the day's immunization clinic. Satisfied, she stood and looked through the doorway to the infirmary.

Everything looked crisp and clean and sparkled in the sunlight that burst through the tall windows on the east side of the building. The clinic was equipped with modern conveniences yet the high ceilings and white crown molding retained the New England architectural feel of the room. Abby absolutely loved it. As a matter of fact, she loved everything about this campus.

She stepped into the hospital. The faint smell of antiseptic assured her the room was recently cleaned. She smiled at the thought of Sam in the clinic. At ten o'clock, twenty four ninth grade students—eleven boys and thirteen girls—would drag in for tetanus boosters. Abby placed her hand on her hip and scanned the room one final time. Everything was in place and ready to go.

She looked at the clock. Six minutes 'til nine, plenty of time for a coffee break before the kids began to arrive.

A flash of past coffee breaks with Robert slid across her mind. At least two or three times a week he stopped by the hospital where she worked and hung around until she was free. They liked to linger over coffee and talk about everything and yet nothing in particular. They were so in love, at least she was, and she thought he loved her too. How could she have been so wrong about him?

When she told him she couldn't live with him until they were married, she thought he'd honor her decision and marry her. He said he would always love her. In reality, he tossed her aside. She viewed herself as used, dirty, and soiled. The picture she allowed him to project on her lasted years.

She shook the memories from her head and stepped into the cafeteria. The aroma of freshly baked bread, and what was that other smell? Roast beef-wafted over her, tempted her senses, and made her stomach growl. The empty tables were spaced around the expansive dining hall. They faced the ceiling-to-floor windows that faced the tennis courts. Four girls and a couple of boys sat at a table in the center of the room with open books in front of them. They horsed around, their banter punctuated with laughter.

She paused and watched their antics, then stepped up to the counter and pushed the spigot on the coffee carafe. Steam curled and rose as she filled her cup and added a liberal amount of half-and-half. She took a sip and savored the creamy robust taste. Sam sat at table in the corner so she headed toward him.

"Hmmph. Cereal. That's not a breakfast for a big strong man like you," a gray-haired lady said to Sam as Abby walked up and set her cup down. A plate of scrambled eggs, bacon, and two pancakes sat in front of him.

"Hi." He glanced at her. "I'm trying to convince Florence that I've already eaten breakfast." He gave her a half grin that made Abby's heart race and sent heat to her cheeks.

"Having a puny bowl of cereal two hours ago doesn't constitute a healthy breakfast." The woman shook her finger at the young man but her smile softened the gesture.

"Abby, this is Florence, the best cook in the country. And Florence, this is Abby, our new nurse."

Florence pulled a towel from her shoulder, wiped her hands, then extended one hand to Abby. A wide smile spread over her wrinkled face as she placed a rough palm next to Abby's.

"I've been trying to tell Florence I can look out for myself. But, as you'll soon learn, you can't argue with Florence...and win that is."

"Pay him no mind," Florence said, and dismissed his comment with a wave of her hand. "It's good to have you here Abby. Now, have a seat and we'll get acquainted. Can I get you anything?"

"Oh, no. Coffee will be enough. But thanks, anyway."

"Are you from around here?" Florence pulled out a chair and sat down.

"No. I recently moved here from Orlando."

"My brother lived there for a couple years," Sam said, his hand in mid-air with a forkful of pancake.

She smiled at him. He might not need this second breakfast but he seemed to enjoy it.

"What brought you here?" Florence asked.

"Let's just say, I needed the change."

"Florence likes to find out everything about everyone here." He smiled at the older woman and raised a brow.

The cook wrinkled her nose at him and smacked him lightly on the arm. "I'm curious is all."

"It's okay." Abby tossed a smile Florence's way. "I can relate."

"I hope you'll stay with us awhile," Florence said. "Seems like we get a nurse, get to know her, and she up and leaves us."

"Not me, I plan to be here for a long time."

"I'm glad to hear that, aren't you, Sam?"

He nodded as he shoveled in the last bite of his breakfast and swallowed as he got out of the chair. "If you ladies will excuse me, I need to get back to work."

"I made your favorite lunch," Florence called after him. "Roast beef."

He turned around and shook his head and put his hands on his belly. "You're going to be the death of me." He shot Abby a wink. "Florence's goal in life is to fatten me up."

"Go on, get out of here." The old cook made shooing motions with her hands. "Just be back for lunch," she called to him before he pushed through the door. She looked toward Abby. "Besides, my goal in life is to get him married off to a good woman, and fatten him up."

Heat shot to Abby's cheeks. "I better head back too. I've got a herd of kids scheduled for shots this morning."

"It was nice meeting you." Florence pushed her chair back and stood. Just as quickly, she sat back down and put her head in her hands.

"Are you okay?" Abby walked around the table and put a hand on the cook's shoulder.

"Just a little dizzy spell. It'll pass."

"Has this happened before?"

Florence nodded.

"How long has it been going on?"

"Couple of days."

"Why don't you come down to my office and let me check you out?"

"Oh, I'll be alright. See, it's already gone." She stood as if for emphasis, but Abby noted the pallor of her cheeks and the slight stumble backward.

"You can't just ignore it. Your body's doing its best to tell you something."

"No need to fuss over me, really."

She put an arm around the older woman's shoulder. "I'm serious. If this continues, you can't ignore it. Promise me, if it happens again you'll come see me, okay?"

"If it gets worse, I'll let you know." Florence smiled. "Now, go see about those kids and stop fretting over me. I'm fine."

"If you say so." Abby walked the short distance

to the clinical area. She had just walked in her office when a girl approached, looking timid as she picked up the clipboard and wrote her name on the sign-in sheet.

Abby read the data upside down. Name: Brenda Arlington. Reason for visit: Talk.

"Come in and have a seat." Abby motioned to the girl who was visibly uncomfortable. She perched on the edge of a chair.

Abby was sure it was concern she saw in the girl's pretty blue eyes. "Now, Brenda, what can I do for you?"

"Well…I'm supposed to get a tetanus shot later this morning and I was wondering…"

Abby paused and waited for the girl to gather her thoughts enough to elaborate. After a few seconds, it appeared no thoughts were forming so she took the initiative.

"Wondering what, hon?"

"If someone is pregnant, would it hurt for them to get the shot?"

Abby tried not to show emotion. "No, not at all. The tetanus booster isn't a live virus." Abby looked into the fourteen-year-old girl's eyes. "Do you think you're pregnant?"

Her face brightened and she shrugged. She pulled a pack of birth control pills from her purse and shoved them across the desk. Her eyes welled with tears. "I don't know. Sometimes I forget to take them."

Abby patted her arm. "Does your mom know you're on the pill?"

"Yes. She got them for me."

Abby breathed a little easier. One less thing she'd have to keep from the girl's mother. Federal law mandated she keep everything confidential; reveal nothing to parents. Abby had no choice. She didn't like it, but it was the law.

The girl squirmed in her chair. "Can I please have a pregnancy test?"

Abby nodded, yes.

Abby guided her to the bathroom and handed her a plastic cup. "When you're finished, leave it on the counter and have a seat in my office. I'll be right with you." She patted the student's shoulder.

Five minutes later, Abby slipped into her desk chair across from Brenda who looked a little lost. "It was negative." Abby reached across and squeezed the girl's hand. "You're not pregnant."

Brenda blew out a sigh. "Thank goodness." She strummed her fingers on the desk. "Then why am I...?"

Abby handed the pills back to her and the girl tucked them inside her purse.

Before Abby got another word out, the girl got up to leave.

"I gotta go," she said as she shot out of her seat. "You won't tell anyone, right?"

"Scout's honor." Abby watched the girl walk away. She shook her head. Little girls playing women. If they only knew...

A few minutes later the students swarmed in ready as they'd ever be for their shots. The girls giggly, the boys rowdy and trying to act like he-men in front of them. She wasn't fooled one bit. They were just as apprehensive about getting the vaccination as the girls were.

Things went smoothly until the last young man. "Okay, Brian, let's get you done and back to class." Abby kept her voice light and cheerful. She could tell the boy was afraid.

She was as swift with him as all the others but when she was done, he didn't look relieved, he looked pale. He's going to pass out on me, Abby thought, and glanced toward the door. Though only fourteen, the husky boy towered over her and if he went down, she would need help. She took him by the arm and helped him sit on one of the exam tables. She stepped to the sink, filled a paper cup with water, and wet a towel to place on his forehead.

When she turned around, he had a hand to his mouth and was trying to scoot off the table. But it was too late. He retched.

* * *

Sam glided his push broom across the floor in the commons area, only half-aware of the chatter of the kids moving about between classes. He mused over the impending meeting with Mrs. Pringle. The assistant dean wasn't the warmest woman he'd ever met and his gut tensed at the very thought. He went over and over in his mind what he would say. He had to say everything just right.

"Mr. Ford." Jeff, a ninth grader, busted toward him and interrupted Sam's reverie.

"Hey, slow down," Sam said, as the boy skidded to a stop just inches from him.

"The nurse needs you."

Sam's heart jerked. "She okay?"

Jeff nodded. "Brian Carrington just barfed all over the place." He shook his head. "I had to go back to the clinic to get my notebook and you should have seen him…"

"Thanks. I'm on it." Sam stepped briskly down the hall to the utility closet, scooted the mop bucket on his supply cart and headed toward the clinic.

When he got to the infirmary, Brian was supine on a clean exam table. Abby stood over him, wiping his brow with a moist towel.

"What happened?" Sam stood beside Abby and looked down at the boy.

"He just got a little sick after I gave him a shot."

"Is he breathing okay? Any signs of anaphylactic shock?"

A frown creased Abby's brow. She looked at him with a combination of annoyance and curiosity. "No. None."

Sam reached out, took Brian's wrist and felt for a pulse. His heartbeat was a little fast but strong and regular, his breathing not labored. Most likely a case of old-fashioned fright.

"His blood pressure and pulse are both fine." She gave him a gaze that questioned his actions.

As he changed his modus operandi from doctor to janitor, he stepped back to let Abby take care of the patient. She checked Brian's BP again. Nurse Dennison was definitely thorough.

"You're doing just fine, Brian." Abby squeezed the excess air out of the cuff. "How's your stomach?"

"I'm okay now. I guess I ate something bad for breakfast."

Sam chuckled. "I wouldn't say that where Florence can hear you. She'll take a broom to you for suggesting anything is wrong with her food."

The boy grinned and Sam could see the tension ease from his face. "I'm sorry I made such a mess."

"Don't worry about the mess. Let's just make sure you're okay." Abby helped Brian sit up. "Are you dizzy?"

He shook his head. "I feel fine now. Really." He scooted from the table.

"I guess you're good to go then." Abby signed her name to a pass and handed it to the boy.

Brian took the pass. "Thanks." He slipped through the door.

A few minutes later, as Sam waited for the mopped floor to dry, he plopped down in a chair by Abby's desk. "That catastrophe is over."

She nodded, and then chuckled.

Abby's laugh was contagious and he quelled the urge to laugh along. Her green eyes sparkled. A delicate heart-shaped face reminded him of Vivian Leigh from the old black and whites he so enjoyed. She had her honey blond hair pulled back in a ponytail. It made her button nose stand out. Suddenly, his chest tugged with emotion.

"What's so funny?"

"Brian. You should have seen him. He literally turned green. Poor kid, I should have known he was nauseated. I thought he was gonna faint on me."

"You never see it coming," Sam said, remembering some of his experiences in the ER. He stood. "Well, the floor's probably dry by now." He stepped back into the infirmary, Abby followed close behind.

He sprayed the exam table with disinfectant mist and wiped it clean. "Looks like you're back to normal now." He stripped off the latex gloves and tossed them in the trash.

"Yeah, thanks for all your help." Abby took a step closer to him. "Let me take a look at that hand, see if it's healing." She took his right hand in hers, turning it palm up. She removed the dressing and skimmed her fingertip under the blistered area. "This is healing nicely. If you wear gloves when you're working, you can leave it uncovered now."

"I keep them right here." He motioned toward the work gloves on his cart. "I always try to be a good patient."

Her full lips turned up at the corners and she gazed directly into his eyes. "You're one of my best patients."

She looked provocative. A smile lit up her face and she had a mischievous glint in her eyes. He reached out and took hold of her hand. She pulled her hand away ever so gently and took a step back.

He said goodbye and left her office. He wondered if he'd done something wrong. But there wasn't time to ponder as he arrived at the assistant dean's door.

Sam walked into Mrs. Pringle's private office and pulled the door closed behind him. His eyes immediately focused on his daughter. He gave her a tentative smile, hopeful for a little encouragement. Predictably, she sent a fierce glare. Linda, seated to

Sara's right, kept her gaze forward.

"Have a seat, Mr. Ford." Mrs. Pringle motioned to the chair on Sara's left across from her desk. She pushed her black-rimmed glasses up her nose and smiled at Sam. "We have a few papers to sign today in order to get things legalized for you and Sara. I understand you will be Sara's guardian, is that correct?"

The gloomy sky released sheets of rain on the window behind Mrs. Pringle and reflected the mood that radiated from Sara and her mother. Sam looked at Linda then back to Mrs. Pringle. "Yes, but…"

Linda scowled at him then raised an eyebrow. "Just sign the papers, Sam. We can talk more about this later." She smiled sweetly at Mrs. Pringle. "No need to take up a lot of this lady's time. I'm sure she has plenty of other things to do today."

Sam glanced at Sara. She stared downward. Her lips pulled tightly together, she gently tapped a toe on the hardwood floor. Sam's gaze shifted to the papers Mrs. Pringle scooted across the desk. At the top of page one, "Longtime friend of the family," jumped out at him. Sam shook his head.

Linda tried to continue the farce. Why did she have to be so difficult? Sam leveled a look at Mrs. Pringle. "Could we," he said, and pointed toward Linda and Sara, "please have a few minutes in private before I sign these?"

Brows drawn together, the assistant dean scooted her chair back and stood. "Certainly. I'll step into the hall. Let me know when you're ready for me."

When the door closed behind Mrs. Pringle, Sara spoke first. "Please Dad, don't tell her you're my father. You promised."

Sam raked fingers through his hair and sucked in a breath. "I know I did sweetheart." He took her damp, warm hand in his. "But when I made that promise I didn't consider the consequences it would have. I *am* your father and lying about it isn't right. I've been praying for God's guidance and leading in this situation and…"

"Praying?" Linda interrupted him. "Please spare us the dramatics. You're saying you had to pray in order to decide if it's okay or not to keep a promise you made to your daughter?" She tossed her head to the side and glowered at him.

Sam sighed. "Linda, when I made that promise I wasn't a Christian. I am now and that changes things." He looked at Sara who had pulled her hand from his. "Honey, please try to see my point."

"Dad…" Sara's eyes filled with tears and spilled over. "Why are you doing this to me? I trusted you to keep one simple promise. Now you're backing out." She sniffed and ran a hand under her nose "You're going to ruin my life."

Sam pulled a tissue from the box on the desk and handed it to Sara. He searched for words. "Sara, I love you. I would never deliberately do anything to hurt you. For weeks I've wrestled with my conscience and no matter how I try, I can't justify the lies. All I want to do is what's best for you." He rubbed his jaw and looked into his daughter's sad eyes. "All I want in this world is your happiness."

Linda leaned toward Sara and said, "I warned you, didn't I? I knew he would be unreasonable about this." She shot an irritated look in Sam's direction.

Sam gathered all the strength he could muster and ignored Linda's attitude. Now was not the time to confront her.

He placed his hand on Sara's shoulder. "We can't continue lying, honey. I regret making a promise I can't keep. At the time I made it, I thought it would be okay. But it's not okay. Deceit is wrong. I'm just sorry it took me so long to finally figure that out." He put both hands on the sides of Sara's tear stained cheeks and turned her face toward him. "We have to tell Mrs. Pringle the truth. Please, Sara, try to understand."

"No!" Sara jerked back. "I'll never understand. Never."

The murmur of the air-conditioning unit and the pounding of rainwater that flowed over the window behind Mrs. Pringle's desk were the only audible sounds for several seconds.

Linda looked at her watch and broke the silence. "I'm getting that woman back in here. I have an appointment in an hour and if we don't get this over with I'm going to be late." She stood and stomped to the door. "I can't believe how selfish you're being," she shot over her shoulder as she grabbed the doorknob. "Why can't you just do what you're supposed to for once in your life?"

Sara blew her nose and tossed the tissue in the trash. The disappointed look she leveled on Sam hit him like a knife to the chest, knocked the wind out of him. *I don't want to hurt Sara, Lord. Please comfort her heart.*

When Mrs. Pringle stepped back into the office a

frown crimped her brow and she gave Sam a quick look. She tucked her hair behind her ear and scooted into the chair behind her desk. "Okay, are we ready to get the papers signed?" Her eyes darted between Sam and Linda.

Sam gathered in a long breath, leaned toward Mrs. Pringle and said, "Let me start at the beginning."

Thirty minutes later, explanations to a shocked Mrs. Pringle were over and the papers signed, Sam headed slowly down the hall. His talk with Mike, the school's Chaplin, crossed his mind. Yesterday morning he confessed everything to his friend and mentor. Mike both counseled and prayed with him. Sam had walked away from the meeting with the knowledge there was only one thing he could do as a Christian. He had to tell the truth. He felt good about his decision at the time. Why had doubts crept in now?

Sam shook the thoughts aside, stepped into the walk-in utility closet and pulled the door closed behind him. He plopped down on the step stool, rested his elbows on his knees and dropped his head into his hands. He wondered if Sara would ever forgive him for his broken promise. A stupid promise based on deceit, one he should never have made in the first place.

"God, I did what I thought was right." He released a heavy breath. If the truth was supposed to set him free, why did he feel so miserable?

CHAPTER FOUR

Friday morning Abby sat down at her desk and scanned the calendar. She noted a ten o'clock staff meeting. She wanted to be prepared to give an accurate report if called on, so she jotted down a short summary of her nursing activities for the past week and slid the notes to the front of her desk.

She idly rotated the pen between her thumb and forefinger, rested her chin on the palm of her other hand and let her thoughts drift to tomorrow's riding lesson. She'd never been on a horse, and she was nervous about getting on such a large animal. Sam would definitely have his job cut out for him.

Oh, Sam, she thought and released a long breath. She remembered the bewildered look on his face when she pulled away from him. She knew she confused him but she made a commitment to herself and God to not have a physical relationship again, and she didn't trust herself to stay faithful to her promise.

A soft knock interrupted her thoughts and she

turned. Clark Wilson, the thirty-something history professor she'd met earlier in the week, stood in the open doorway. Dressed in a red and white pin-striped shirt that complimented his neatly groomed sandy brown hair, he looked every bit the professor.

"Got a minute?"

"Sure, come in." She laid the pen down and smiled.

"I'm not disturbing you, am I?" He walked to her desk.

"Not at all." She tucked her hair behind her ear and looked into his intense hazel eyes. "Have a seat." She gestured to the chair beside her desk. "What can I do for you this morning?"

Clark slid into the seat. "I scraped my finger on a rusty nail last night. Nothing serious, but it did break the skin. I'm not positive but I think I'm due for a tetanus booster. Could you check for me?"

"Sure, I can do that." Her fingers slid across the keyboard, deftly typing his name. The screen popped up. "Let's see. Your last one was six years ago. Since you have a scratch I'll go ahead and boost you."

"Okay," Clark said, but his tone indicated it was anything but okay, and she suppressed the urge to laugh.

She went to get the shot. "I'll just be a minute."

"No need to hurry." He chuckled. "I'll be right here."

While she drew up the medicine, she could here Clark shuffle in his seat. Some men were such babies.

When she returned to her desk, Clark had his

sleeve pushed up. She gave him the vaccine and covered the small hole with a smiley face Band-Aid. "All set."

"Thanks." He stood and walked toward the door, paused for a moment, then turned around and said, "I'm going to grab a cup of coffee in the cafeteria before my next class. Would you care to join me?"

Abby looked at her watch. "Sounds great."

Less than two minutes later, they were seated at a table in the back of the dining hall, sipping coffee. "I'm glad it's Friday. I'm ready for the weekend."

"Me, too."

"How did your first week go?" He sat the cup down and ran his finger around the rim.

"Really well."

"All settled in, then?"

"Yep, I've got the routine down pretty well, I think."

Clark was about to say something when Abby's phone rang. She hesitated, cell phone etiquette was such a gray area.

"Go ahead," he said. "It could be important."

"Thanks." She pulled the phone from her scrubs and looked at the caller ID. "Hey Emily. What's up?"

"Not much. I thought I'd have lunch with my big sister today if you're free, check out your new facility."

"That'll be great." Abby smiled and wrinkled her nose. "Don't you work today?"

Emily chuckled. "I'm taking a personal day."

"Okay, I'll see you later. Drive safe." Abby ended the call and slipped the phone back into her pocket. She looked at Clark. "That was my sister, Emily, who lives in Orlando. She will be here for lunch."

"In this rain?" Clark motioned toward the expansive glass doors where a downpour pelted against the panes. "It's an hour's drive on a good day."

She sighed. "Maybe the rain will ease up by the time she heads out. But, even if it doesn't, you don't know my little sister." Abby chuckled and reached for her mug. "A little storm never stopped her from anything."

"She's quite the adventurer, huh?"

"Yes, she's that all right." Her thoughts turned to Emily's last visit on Monday and the questions she asked about Robert. She seemed so concerned about Abby. Then on Tuesday, out of the blue, Robert called. She hadn't heard from him in months. He was chipper and inquisitive, chatted away like it was the norm. It reminded her of the days when they were still together. He could be quite the charmer, but she cautioned herself to remember he was the past.

"…And I've been here ten years now."

Clark's words seeped into her brain and snapped her back to the present. "You must like it here, then."

"I do. It's a lot different from the public school system. With only 120 students, I know all the kids by name and it didn't take long to learn their personalities. You don't get that personal connection with a mainstream campus." He tipped up his mug and took a drink. "I don't plan to ever leave Brighton."

"I can see myself here for the duration, too." She glanced at her watch. "Oops, gotta go."

She took the last drink from her cup, swallowed while she scooted back her chair, and stood. She motioned toward Clark's injection site. "Exercise that arm so it won't get sore."

He smiled. "Will do...hey, I had a great time. Maybe we can do it again sometime."

"Sure, sounds great."

* * *

The downpour hadn't eased up one bit by noon when Emily appeared in the doorway clad in a raincoat and clutching a partially closed umbrella that dripped water on the floor.

"I should have brought a boat." Emily leaned the umbrella against the wall, then shrugged out of her coat and hung it on a peg behind the door. "I'm not late, am I? The rain really slowed me down."

"No. It's just a couple minutes after twelve. I don't know about you, but I'm starved. Come on, let's go." Abby took her sister's arm and guided her down the hall.

The cafeteria was packed with students and staff and hummed with activity. They got in line for the buffet. It looked like they were the last of the lunch group if the full tables and sparse selection were any indication.

Abby scooped up a chicken breast smothered in a creamy sauce and put it on her plate.

"Your school is really swanky." Emily pointed to

her tray. "This sure isn't the hamburger hash they used to sling at us at Orlando High."

"Yeah." Abby winked. "If I'm not careful, I'm going to pack on the pounds."

"With your metabolism, not a chance." Emily wrinkled her nose. When she reached for a piece of fish her hand trembled a little.

"You okay, Em?"

Emily darted her head toward Abby. "Why?"

"You seem like you're about to jump out of your skin, that's why."

"You sound like mom." Emily rolled her eyes like only a little sister could. "When did you start using phrases like 'jump out of your skin?'"

Abby shrugged. "I don't know, maybe when I grew up."

"Touché." Emily rolled her eyes again.

Abby scanned the packed dining hall as she balanced her tray. "Looks like all the tables are taken."

"What now?" Emily asked.

"There's Sam." He sat at a table in the far corner and motioned to the sisters. "Come on, follow me." She guided Emily across the cafeteria.

"That's him?" Emily whispered.

"Shh."

"Hi, Sam. This is my sister, Emily Dennison. Em, this is Sam Ford."

He stood and extended a hand. "Nice to meet you, Emily."

"Ditto," Emily said and shook his hand. "Is it always this crowded in here?"

"No, not when it's nice out. The rain brought

everyone inside today. You two can sit here, I'm finished."

"Are you sure?" Abby said. "We could eat in my office."

"I'm positive. I was about to leave when you came in. I knew you'd never find an empty table." Sam tossed her a wink. "So I just waited and saved this one for you."

"Thank you." She looked into his eyes and smiled. "What a sweet thing to do."

His ears grew pink and he looked away. "Have a nice lunch, ladies."

Emily watched Sam walk away and blew out an audible breath. "You're right, McDreamy's got nothing on that guy." She set her tray on the table and slid into a chair. "I'm surprised someone hasn't already snatched him up."

"Go figure."

Emily cocked her head to the side. "Have you had any more dates with him?"

Abby shook her head and smiled at her inquisitive sister. "No, not yet. But did I mention he's going to give me a riding lesson in the morning?"

Emily took a bite. Her eyes twinkled as she ate, then her eyebrows shot up. "No! You didn't! Abby, that's awesome. What? Are you holding out on me now?"

Abby laughed and lifted her shoulders. "Would I dare to keep anything from you?"

"You better not." Emily leveled a look at Abby. "You call me the minute you get home tomorrow and fill me in. I want all the details, okay?"

"Cross my heart." She grinned. Being with her sister always caused her to revert to childhood. Why was that?

She cut into her smothered chicken. "How's Boo Boo? Is she excited about graduation?" They'd given their younger sister, Carrie, that nickname early on as she was an unexpected, but happy, surprise to their forty-year-old mother. The name stuck all these years.

"You know Boo Boo, everything excites her."

Abby nodded as she swallowed a bite. "I can't believe our baby sister is going off to college in the fall. Is Mom dealing with that okay?"

"I think so. If she's not, she'd never admit it. But I'm afraid she's going to have one big case of empty-nest-syndrome. Even though I'm still living at home, it won't set well with her when her baby moves out."

Abby laid down her fork. "Yeah, I know. Her last child leaving home will hit her hard. We should take her to Disney World that weekend to get her mind on something else."

"Yep, like you and me for a change." Emily blew out an exaggerated sigh.

In all fairness to their mother, Carrie's birth had not only taken them by surprise, but Mom was able to be the mother in middle age she felt she'd never been in youth. So naturally, Carrie was a bit spoiled. It never bothered Abby, but Emily always felt abandoned.

Abby looked at the sister who frequently turned to her for nurturing. "So what do you think? Just you, Mom, me, and Mickey Mouse of course."

Emily laughed. "It'll be fun. We can make the whole weekend of it. I'll let Dad know our plans ahead of time so he can arrange some serious golfing with his friends."

"He'll like that."

Emily tapped on her phone. "It's on my calendar."

"Okay, that's settled." Abby pushed her plate back and pulled the glass of lemonade toward her. "You'll never guess who called me Tuesday."

"Who? Sam?"

"No, not Sam." She looked directly into Emily's eyes. "Robert."

"Oh yeah." Emily pulled her brows together and straightened her shoulders. "What did he want?"

Abby shrugged. "Who knows? He said he just called to see how I'm doing, but I didn't buy into that for one minute." Abby ran her fingers around the edge of her glass. "He did ask about you."

"Me?" Emily shifted in her seat, and hitched in a breath. "What in the world did he want to know about me?"

"He asked when I'd last seen you. I found that a little odd. Don't you?"

"Yeah, odd." Emily stuffed the last bite of fish into her mouth, swallowed and dabbed her mouth with a napkin. She scooted her chair back. "How about giving me a tour of the school?"

She stared at Emily's too-innocent face. Her sister definitely changed the subject. But why?

****

At four-thirty in the afternoon, Sam wheeled his supply cart into the utility room. It wouldn't be long until dinner with his daughter. Linda planned to drop her off at six, and he'd take her back to Linda's at nine. Would this be the last weekend she'd get to spend with her mom?

The thought of seeing Sara tugged at his heart, and threatened to yank it out. He hadn't talked with her since they met with Mrs. Pringle two days ago. He prayed his little girl was okay, and had accepted his decision to end all the lies. He raked a hand through his hair. A knot twisted in his gut as he envisioned Sara, so young and vulnerable, now tossed into the throes of adult issues. But kids are resilient. Didn't they pop back quickly? Fat chance. Not when you have a mother who abandons you, and a father who breaks promises.

Sam dumped the mop bucket, rinsed it and turned it upside down in the sink. He peeled off the latex gloves and looked at his palm. It was almost healed. Thoughts of Abby flashed through his mind and he smiled. He needed an excuse to see her. He decided to stop by her office on the way home and confirm the riding lesson.

Five minutes later, he stood in front of Abby's office. He knocked. She opened the door and his pulse leaped. White Capri slacks hugged her slim hips and her green and white striped knit top brought out the lime-colored flecks in her eyes. She looked fabulous. When he found himself focused a second too long on the appealing softness of her lips, he forced himself to speak. "Hi."

"Hi yourself." A blush tinted her cheeks.

"Are you ready to leave?"

"Not quite. Come on in." She turned and led the way to where she needed to finish her work.

"Can't stay but a minute." Sam sidled up to her desk and lowered himself into a chair. "Are you all set for your lesson tomorrow? Or have you backed out on me?" He grinned and winked.

Her eyes sparkled. "No chance. I'm ready for this."

"Good. I was afraid you'd be nervous."

"I am a little nervous. But mostly excited."

"You'll do fine. Trust me."

"I do trust you. Otherwise I wouldn't be getting on a half-ton animal per your instructions." She laughed.

He gave her a slow grin, savoring her enthusiasm. "The thunderstorms have moved out of the area so we won't have to use the covered pen."

"Yeah." Abby chuckled. "The rain stopped just about the time Emily made it back to Orlando."

Sam looked at Abby's features, her firm, high cheekbones and long curled eyelashes that framed her perfect emerald green eyes. Her shoulder length blond hair tumbled forward around her tanned face. "I can see the resemblance between you and your sister."

"We hear that a lot."

"You two are close, aren't you?"

"Yes." She smiled. "I was seven when Emily was born. I was the bossy older sister. Now, she's my closest friend."

"I can relate. My older brother and I are best buds. What about your youngest sister? Does she look like the two of you?"

Abby shook her head. "Not at all. Carrie's petite and five feet tall. She has dark hair and brown eyes. She looks like our dad, except for the height."

"Does she live in Orlando?"

"Yeah. She's still at home, but not for long. She graduates high school in two weeks."

"Off to college, then?"

"Uh huh. She starts at St. Petersburg Community in the fall."

"Let me guess. She's going to be in the medical field like her older sister."

"She hasn't decided yet, but she has plenty of time to make up her mind." Abby leaned back in her swivel chair. "You mentioned college before, where did you go?"

"Atlanta, then Chicago." Sam cleared his throat and switched positions. He needed to steer her away from this subject. Chicago was where he completed his medical internship and he didn't want to get into that with her, not now.

"So how's it going?" he said. "Are you getting acquainted with the staff?"

If she noticed the abrupt subject change she didn't let on. "Yes. Some of the teachers dropped by and introduced themselves. I met the rest of the faculty at the staff meeting this morning." She chuckled. "Clark made sure I met everyone."

"Clark?"

"Professor Wilson, the history teacher. I had coffee with him before the meeting."

"Oh." A hot wave of jealousy surged up Sam's neck. Why did he feel like she stuck a pin in him, deflating his upbeat mood? It was just coffee, not a real date.

"Are you okay? You look a little flushed."

"I'm fine." He tugged at the collar on his brown work shirt. "I've kept you long enough." Sam pulled himself to his feet. "I'll get out of here so you can finish up and head home."

Abby walked with him to the door. He turned to face her. He wanted to squeeze her hand, but he didn't want to do anything to offend her or scare her off. "See you in the morning."

"Ten o'clock sharp." She tilted her head and looked up at him, her lips turning up at the corners.

Sam returned her smile. His unexpected reaction over Abby's coffee break with the professor surprised him. Was the pretty nurse attracted to Clark? No doubt in his mind, the history professor's interest in her was piqued. He pulled his reflections back to the present and made his way to the parking lot. He slid behind the wheel of his Taurus and drove home.

In his apartment, an hour later, Sam heard the front door open then bang shut. Sara burst into the kitchen. "Let's eat. I've got to get back by eight. The softball tournament starts tonight."

"Everything's ready." He motioned to a chair. "Have a seat."

Sam set the burgers, hot and steaming from the grill, on the table, walked to the refrigerator and pulled out a large bowl of salad. "What kind of dressing do you like?"

"Ranch."

He grabbed the salad dressing and juggled his

handful to the table. Sara didn't have much to say. Every attempt he made at conversation failed. She picked at her food and her eyes darted to the wall clock every few minutes. She was bored and antsy to get the meal over with and get away from him. He knew it by the way she acted. "When is your mom leaving?"

"Two weeks."

"Are you okay with that?"

She shot him a look. "Might as well be. What difference does it make what I think?" She shoved her chair back and took her plate to the sink.

"I made pudding, your favorite. Help yourself, it's in the fridge."

"No thanks." She turned and walked to the door.

Sam cleared the table and put the leftovers in the refrigerator. Dishes could wait; he needed to talk to her. He followed her into the living room and found her petite frame in his oversized recliner. She looked like a toy. A movie played too loudly on the television. "Honey, would you mind to turn it down a notch, please?"

She glared at him and punched the off button, then tossed the remote on the end table. "Better?"

"You didn't have to turn it off. I like the classics."

"Whatever."

Sam took a deep breath and sat on the sofa, facing her. "I know you're upset with me, honey. I'm sorry I hurt you. I never meant…"

She shrugged. "Just forget it. The damage is done."

"Come on, give me a break, work with me here.

I'm trying to get close to you, be a father to you."

"A little late to play daddy, don't you think, after all these years."

"Look, I wish I could have been there for you from the beginning. Believe me I regret I missed so much of your life. But it's not too late for us to build a relationship."

Her face reddened and she glared at him. "Just back off, leave me alone. How can you talk about building a relationship when you can't even keep a promise?" She shot up from her chair. "I hate you," she screamed and bolted down the hall to the bathroom and slammed the door behind her.

Sam shook his head. Had he made a mistake? Is breaking a confidence as bad as concealing something?

Fifteen minutes later, Sara, eyes red and puffy, plopped back into the recliner. Sam's heart swelled as he grasped for words. "Are you okay?"

She nodded.

"I love you, Sara. I hope you believe that."

Silence. She stared straight ahead.

Sam slid his palm across his damp forehead. "So, what do you and your mom have planned for the weekend?"

"Nothing. I'm staying at school."

"I thought you were spending the weekend with Linda."

She shrugged. "Plans change. You should know that."

A sting shot through Sam. "If it's because of the game tonight, you could always go to your mom's tomorrow."

"She's busy packing, okay?"

Sam winced. Had Linda blown her daughter off again? "Since you already have a weekend pass, why not stay here? I have a riding lesson scheduled in the morning, but that's not a problem. You could come with me."

"No way." She shot daggers at him, bent over and picked up her purse. "It's time for me to go, Sam."

CHAPTER FIVE

Abby slipped her purse over a shoulder, and stepped out the sliding glass door into a beautiful, balmy Saturday morning. She breathed in the scent of the bay. The distinct smell of salt water filled her nose. Waves splashed on the beach a hundred feet from her back patio. Already a few of the tenants strolled along the private shoreline. The retired couple who lived above her waved and she waved back. She stood and watched them meander down the beach, hand in hand, barefoot and kicking up sand with each step they took.

Abby loved Florida. She'd lived here most of her life, but this was her first home on the beach. She liked having the ocean only a stone's throw from her back door. Last night she went to bed with her window open. The sound of waves, as they lapped against the shore, lulled her to sleep. Soon she couldn't do that; once the heat came, she would need the air conditioning on.

A breeze teased Abby's hair when she stepped

from the patio and headed toward her Taurus. A horn honked in the distance, drowning out the squawk of a seagull as it swooped down for its breakfast.

She wasn't out of the driveway before her cell phone rang. Her caller ID flashed Emily. Abby smiled. She knew the call was to make sure she didn't oversleep and use it as an excuse to back out of the riding lesson. "Hey, Em. How's my beautiful sister?"

"I'm good, you sound cheerful."

"I am."

"Are you getting ready to meet McDreamy?"

Abby closed her eyes and suppressed a squeal. "I'm sitting in my car, ready to head out as we speak."

"Great. Are you excited?

"Uh huh." All week she had butterflies—a combination of excitement and fear fought for control but excitement won out every time. When she tried to visualize herself on the back of a horse, she got a scary chill down her spine.

"I'd be excited too, if I was going to spend the morning with Adonis."

Abby shook her head, laughed. "You're too funny."

"Don't forget to call me when you get back."

"I won't forget.

"Okay, talk to you later. Have fun."

She loved her new apartment. She felt safe and secure. She hummed while she drove

Her first week at work went well and she was able to get a handle on the routine. Her job at the school was a lot different than her job at Orlando General, certainly less chaotic. She wasn't constantly running into people that knew Robert; that was a plus.

She was at the stables sooner than she expected. She parked on the gravel lot and sat for a moment to take a deep breath and relax. With it came the smell of horses and hay. She smiled.

Sam stood outside the fenced paddock, one foot propped on the bottom rail. He turned and she saw his blue eyes crinkle at the corners when he gave her a wide grin. "Hey, Abby." He slid his boot from the fence and stepped toward her. "You're right on time."

He was dressed in blue jeans, a Polo and Lacers. He looked mighty appealing.

She smiled. "Hi, Sam."

"Ready for your first lesson?" He opened the gate and ushered her in.

"I'm looking forward to it." Abby glanced from Sam to the horses in the paddock, then back to Sam. "I hope I'm a quick learner."

"You'll do great." He guided her to the rear of the paddock.

The trainer stood in one of the stalls and brushed a chocolate brown horse. The animal, a towering giant, stood still, head low and his ears pricked forward.

"Hey, Fred. Remember Abby?" Sam asked.

He nodded. "Nice to officially meet you, miss." He laid the brush on a shelf and wiped his palm on the side of his jeans. "I hear you're ready to learn how to ride."

"I am."

"This is Hero." Fred rubbed the muzzle of the beautiful creature beside him. "He's your riding partner today."

"He?" Abby bit her lower lip and shot a look toward Sam. "Aren't male horses temperamental? I've heard they're hard to control."

Sam shook his head. "Hero is a gelding. In layman's terms, that's a castrated male. Geldings have a calm nature. They are easier to work with than stallions and mares." He gave her a wink. "You don't have a thing to worry about with Hero."

"Okay." Abby took a step forward, still a comfortable distance between her and the horse. She sighed. "He's even bigger up close."

Fred chuckled and stroked the animal's mane. "You're right. He's big. But he's one of the meekest horses here. Isn't that so, Sam?"

"Yep." Sam moved close to her side. "And he loves people."

Abby looked up at him. "Good to know."

"You two are going to get along just fine," Fred said. "He's gentle as a kitten." Fred gave Hero a final stroke. "No need to be afraid of him."

"I'm not afraid." She saw the grin both men tried to suppress their amusement. "Okay, maybe a little, but I'll get over it, I promise."

Fred smiled. "Hero's a pushover for a pretty face. You'll have him wrapped around your little finger in no time."

"I don't doubt that. Hero doesn't stand a chance," Sam said huskily. The piercing look he gave her burned through her and said more than his words implied. Heat rushed to her cheeks as she met his gaze.

A discreet cough from Fred redirected Abby's attention. The trainer grinned, his eyes flicked back and forth between Sam and Abby. "Come on over here and get acquainted with him." Fred motioned toward Hero. "Talk to him, he'll like that. Touch him, let him get used to your scent."

She took a deep breath, exhaled the anxiety that brewed inside and inched forward. She reached up and laid her hand on the horse's neck. It was taut, rippling with muscle. "You're a strong one aren't you?" Somehow, talking to the gelding felt right, natural, like she'd been doing it for years.

She stepped closer and rubbed his nose. Hero snuffled toward her so she held out her hand. His warm soft lips and prickly whiskers tickled her palm. "Hello, boy. I'd really like to be your friend."

Hero nudged her with his big brown head, rubbed his jowl against her shoulder.

"Maybe you're going to like me, too, huh?" she said.

Sam reached out and patted the horse's nose. "He likes to be fussed over."

"I can tell."

"I'll get the riding gear while you two bond." Sam gave Hero's nose a final pat and headed through the door.

As Abby watched him go, her heart fluttered.

She turned and focused on the horse. "He's so pretty. What kind of a horse is he?"

"He's a Paso Fino." Fred slid a hand over the gelding's thick mane. "That's all we train here.

They're one of the smartest breed of horses around. Smart, yet docile. We can't have nervous horses around the students. We want the kids to feel comfortable with them."

"I can understand that." She relaxed a little more. But, she wasn't on Hero's back. Not yet...

* * *

After he gathered the riding gear from the tack room, Sam stepped back into the spacious stall. He leaned one shoulder on the doorframe and watched Abby talk to the gelding as she stroked his cheek. She was a natural with animals.

Sam loved her look, all fresh and exuberant, dressed in jeans and a red T-shirt. Her slim fingers glided over Hero's muzzle. He'd never felt this attracted to a woman before. It wasn't just her looks, although she was definitely blessed with beauty. She was intelligent, intuitive, and sensitive. It was funny how he could bond with her so quickly.

Fred stood next to Abby and watched her interact with Hero, a satisfied smile on his face. He spotted Sam and gave him a thumbs-up gesture.

Sam cleared his throat. "I think it's about time to get this big guy saddled up."

Abby turned toward him, her eyes twinkling with excitement.

"Looks like you and Hero hit it off." Sam slipped the halter over the steed's head, clipped on the lead rope and secured it.

"I really think I did." Abby took a step back to

give Sam room.

Fred cuffed Sam on the shoulder and said, "I'm going to get back to work. If you guys need anything, I'll be in there." He pointed to the tack room. "Have a great ride."

"Thanks for all the advice," Abby called as he walked away.

Sam slid the saddle pad into place and then lowered the saddle onto the gelding's back. The gelding looked at him, but held still. "Horses are perceptive. They sense when someone is gentle. He likes you and knows you'll be good to him. He won't object when you ride him."

"I feel a lot more confident than I thought I would."

"It'll be a snap. Hero has lots of experience with first time riders. He's an old pro." Sam pulled the girth strap tight around the animal's middle.

Abby shifted her feet. "How come we're the only one's here? I figured the place would be really busy today."

"There are at least a half-dozen employees already on the trail." With the bridle securely in place, Sam removed the halter and hooked the lead rope to the snaffle bit. "As for the students, the kids that aren't sleeping in this morning are on weekend passes. Things always pick up around here in the afternoon. That's why I head out early. I get to choose the horse I want. Fred makes sure I get my favorite."

"And which one is that?"

Sam pointed toward the front of the paddock. "See that bluish-gray horse? That's Savannah and I always choose her. She's a mare with a lot of spunk."

"A lot of spunk?" Abby tucked a strand of honey-blond hair behind her ear and wrinkled her nose.

"We get along just fine." Sam knotted the reins and dropped them over the saddle horn. "Ready?"

Abby nodded.

Sam took the lead rope and held it toward her. "I'll let you lead him to the training pen."

"Okay." As she took the rope, her hand touched his and a jolt of excitement flashed through her.

They walked through the gate and across the grass. Sam opened the door to the training pen and Abby led the horse inside the arena.

"Are you glad you made the switch to Brighton?" He let go of the bridle and gave Abby full control of the lead rope.

"I love it here." Abby laughed. "I'm trying hard to remember everyone's name and that's a challenge."

"It takes time." He remembered his first week and how hard he tried to keep everyone's names straight. "But you'll get it."

Abby tossed a glance over her shoulder at the horse, then fixed her gaze on Sam. "I ran in to Mrs. Pringle in the Deli after school Thursday. We had a nice talk."

Had the Assistant Dean mentioned anything to her about Sara? He hoped not. He wanted to be the one to tell her when the time was right. He searched Abby's eyes for a clue.

"Mrs. Pringle can be tough," he said, "but she's

fair. Most of the students appreciate that about her."

"It sounds like she has a lot going on in her personal life."

Sam nodded.

"She mentioned her ill mother and seemed depressed."

"I know, poor soul. She's had a rough time the last couple of months. Her mother isn't doing very well. Early Alzheimer's, I think. Anyway that's what it sounds like. And she's only in her mid-sixties. Mrs. Pringle drives to Miami every weekend to check on her. It'll just be a matter of time until her mother won't be able to live alone."

"Alzheimer's is such a sad disease, for the patient as well as the family."

He shook his head. "I agree."

For several minutes they walked the gelding around the pen, Sam stopped and patted Hero's neck. "Do you want to ride him now?"

Abby tipped her head. "I'd like that." She looked so serious, so determined. Sam had to bite the inside of his lower lip to tamp down a smile.

"Let me show you how to mount a horse. With one foot in the stirrup, Sam swung his right leg up and over the saddle. The creak of leather, the shift of the horse adjusting to his weight felt familiar. He loved riding. He was right at home on the back of a horse.

She put her hands on her hips and eyed him. "You make that look easy."

"It's not hard. Trust me." He dismounted. "Are you ready to give it a try?"

She blew out a breath and stepped beside her

instructor.

He motioned toward the saddle. "Take hold of the saddle horn and put your left foot in the stirrup." When she complied, Sam continued, "Now, you're going to throw your right leg up and over, just like I did." He placed a hand on each side of her waist and gave her a boost.

Abby settled into the saddle and tossed him a wide grin. "I made it."

"You sure did." He unclipped the lead rope, wound it into a circle and slipped it over his shoulder and handed her the reins. "I'll guide him around the arena until you feel comfortable enough to handle him on your own."

Abby shifted her weight and gripped the reins in her hands.

"Okay, here we go." Sam grasped the bridle then stepped forward on the sandy footing of the pen. The horse followed.

"I feel like a rubber ball bouncing up and down. Is the ride always this bumpy?" Her words were choppy.

Sam tossed his head back and laughed. Her cheeks were rosy and she looked like a porcelain doll as she bobbed up and down. "In time, you'll learn to go with the flow, and you won't bounce so much."

"Thank goodness," she said between bobs. "This is everything I ever imagined and even more." She sighed, breathless. "Exhilarating! Exciting!"

"I know, I never tire of riding. Give me a horse in a slow cantor across a field. There's nothing I like better." Sam took his hand from the bridle.

"He's all yours now. Walk him around the arena."

"You'll come too?"

"I'm right with you."

She was terrific. She rode like it was second nature. He relished the light banter they shared as she guided Hero twice around the training pen.

"Your first lesson went well." Sam helped Abby dismount and together they led the horse back to the stable.

"I hope I didn't wear you out," she said. "I got to ride. You had to walk."

Sam shrugged. "The exercise didn't hurt me a bit."

"Are you sure?"

"With the way Florence feeds me? I need to work it off somehow."

"I hear that."

Back in the barn, Sam pulled off the saddle. Hero sauntered to the water trough and dipped his head for a long drink.

"You did great today. Are you sure you haven't been around horses before?"

"Never."

He tipped his head and scrutinized her face. "Honest?"

"Cross my heart." She traced an X on her chest.

"Well, you could have fooled me, the way you took to Hero."

Her eyes twinkled at the compliment. "Why thank you, sir."

Sam could hear the smile in her voice and her coy inflection sent a tingle zipping along his nerve endings. He liked it when she flirted. He tossed her a wink and said, "Want to do this again next Saturday?"

"Yes, I'd like that."

"I'll saddle up Savannah and ride with you."

"Sounds great."

Sam cocked his head to the side. "It's a date then. We'll ride in the arena next week, but the week after I bet you'll be ready for the riding trail."

"Sorry, I can't go the following week. That's the weekend of my baby sister's graduation."

"Okay, how about a rain check?"

"But, I will be anxious to graduate to the riding trail."

He grabbed a *Dandy* brush and motioned for her to join him. He headed toward the horse, who, finished with his drink, came up to the fence. Sam brushed him. He loved the smell of horses and hay. "Fred will let him cool down for at least an hour before he can go out again. The trainers here are exceptional; they take good care of the animals."

"I can see that," she said, and touched his arm. "Thank you for working with me today, for being so patient."

"My pleasure." He looked down at her. She moved her hand, and his arm felt warm and tingly from her touch. "I had a great time this morning."

"Me, too."

He couldn't pull his gaze from her. She looked so vulnerable. He wanted to be honest with her, tell her the truth about Sara. He'd have to do that soon before she heard it from someone else. He wondered how she'd respond when she discovered his deception. Would she forgive him?

Sam blinked and glanced at her feet. "If you're going to do a lot of riding, you might consider boots. They work better in the stirrups and will give you a better grip."

Abby looked down at her New Balance sneakers. "I can do that." Her mouth turned up at the corners. "Well, I'll see you later," she said as she turned to leave.

"Yeah, later." Sam watched her walk away. She stopped at the gate, turned, and waved. He shook his head and smiled. She's quite a woman, he thought as he returned the wave.

Chapter Six

Friday night after Carrie's graduation, Abby settled into a chair between her two sisters in their mom's kitchen. Her mother set a bowl of Jiffy-Pop on the table next to a tray of fresh vegetables and homemade dip. The aroma of fresh-popped corn wafted over Abby and made her stomach rumble. Although Mom fixed a feast before the ceremony, Abby wanted to dig in again.

Her dad assembled a plate of snacks and headed to the family room to catch the end of a baseball game. Her father loved his ball games, especially when the Tampa Rays was involved.

Carrie reached for a carrot stick and raked it through the dip. She elbowed Abby. "So, tell us about this guy in your life."

"What guy?" She made her eyes go wide and feigned innocence.

"Oh come on! Em says all you talk about is what's-his-name that's giving you riding lessons." Carrie pushed out her lower lip. "I'm not a baby;

don't leave me out of the good stuff."

Abby breathed out. "Okay, fine, his name is Sam Ford." Abby paused to let the janitor's face slide across her mind. "There's not a whole lot to tell. He's a great guy and I enjoy spending time with him."

"And he's gorgeous," Emily added.

"Oh yeah." Abby smiled. "He's definitely handsome."

Mom shrugged and palmed a handful of popcorn. "I think Emmy has someone special in her life, but she's keeping him a big secret."

"I am not." Emily leveled a look at Mom.

"Are too," Carrie said. "And we don't even know the mystery man's name."

Emily's face brightened. "When, and if, there's an announcement to make, you guys will be the first to know. So, can we just drop it please?"

Abby wondered why Emily was so flustered. She acted strange lately, jumpy about everything. If she met a guy, why was she so closed-mouthed? It wasn't like her to keep things from her family, especially her older sister.

"So can you actually ride a horse now?" Carrie abruptly changed the subject.

"Believe it or not, I can." Abby laughed. "And I love it."

Dad came back into the kitchen with a wide grin spread across his face. He was six-foot-three and all muscle. He didn't look his sixty years. "The Rays won, four to three."

"All right!" Carrie high-fived him.

Dad pulled out a chair and sat down. For the next

hour, he made them laugh with stories of their childhood antics. Many of them Abby hadn't thought of in years. She loved time with her parents and siblings. It made her all warm and cozy. Unlike Emily, who never left the nest, Abby had been on her own since college. Though she liked her independence, the little girl in her cherished times like these, when the world included only her and her family.

Later, after their mom and dad went to bed, Abby and her sisters headed to Carrie's room where they slid into sleeping bags on the floor.

"Just like old times, a pajama party," Carrie said. "I'm glad you came home for my graduation, Abby."

"I wouldn't have missed it for anything."

Carrie grinned and eyed both sisters. "Thanks for the scrapbook, it's so neat. I should've known you guys were up to something." She laughed. "Every time I turned around, Em had her camera out."

"Mom gave me most of the pictures I needed," Abby said, "but I wanted some of your last few months before graduation."

"Well it's the best gift ever. I love it! You guys did a lot of work."

"Abby did the hard part." Emily took a long drink. "All I did was get the pictures to her."

A wide yawn stretched Carrie's face and she covered it with a palm. "Don't let me sleep past ten in the morning. I'm having lunch with Jeff's family."

"How are things with you and Jeff?" Abby asked. Her youngest sister dated Jeff all through high school. Carrie only dated one guy before Jeff and that didn't last long.

"Great. I'll miss him when he leaves for Alabama this fall. But we'll keep in touch. We decided to see other people while we're in college."

Abby was proud of her sister's smart choices. She was always the level-headed sibling. "Good decision, Boo Boo."

"Eww." Carrie batted Abby with a pillow. "Will you guys ever stop calling me that?"

"Never." Abby and Emily said in unison and then giggled.

Carrie shot her sisters a look. "Are you guys ever going to treat me like an adult? I'm not just your kid sister anymore. Good grief, I'm eighteen."

"Doesn't matter." Abby rested her elbow on a pillow and propped her chin on her hand. "You're always going to be our little Boo Boo." A smile tugged at the corners of Carrie's mouth. She loved being the baby of the family.

"Okay, fess up Abby. What exactly is going on with you and Sam?" Emily arranged herself in the bag, apparently not all talked out.

Abby gathered a breath. "I really like him. I haven't felt like this in a long time. It kinda scares me."

"I hope he doesn't turn out to be like Robert," Carrie said, her eyelids droopy.

"Don't worry, Carrie. He's nothing like Robert," Abby answered.

Emily shot Carrie a sharp look, then turned toward Abby. "I'm happy for you, Abs. It's about time you focused on someone other than Robert."

Abby nodded. "Robert isn't a Christian and the Bible warns us not to be unequally yoked with an unbeliever. So it was a mistake to date him, I should have known better. My second mistake…"

"Don't go there. Leave it in the past." Emily adjusted her pillow. "Just be happy for what you have now."

"I am," Abby said, and rubbed her palms together. She glanced at Carrie. "Boo Boo conked out."

"Yep, it's been a long day for her." Emily scooted out of her sleeping bag and motioned toward the door. "Let's go to my room so we won't disturb her."

Abby shrugged out of the warm bag and hooked her arm through Emily's. They tiptoed down the hall and entered the room on the right, and plopped down cross-legged on the bed.

"Abby, there's something I need to talk to you about." Emily's voice turned serious, a frown cut her forehead.

"What is it, Em? Is something wrong?"

"It's about Robert."

"Robert!" Abby shook her head. "I don't want to think about him. Like you said, he's in the past."

"For you." Emily pressed her lips together. "But not for me."

Abby drew her brows together and gave her sister a fleeting look. "You? What's Robert got to do with you?"

"Well… I've been, like sorta seeing him."

"You're kidding, right?"

Emily shook her head.

"He's a user, you know that."

"Oh, Abs, he's not a bad guy. He's just not the right person for you."

Abby sat straight, shoulders back. She didn't want to believe what she heard. Her jaw dropped, but she couldn't speak.

"Please don't be mad at me. I never meant for it to happen. I ran in to him about six months ago at the mall. We talked and had coffee. After that…well, things just developed."

Abby stared at her, dumbstruck.

"Don't look at me like that. Say something, anything."

The magnitude of her sister's betrayal washed over her, drowning any hopes that she misunderstood this conversation. Emily's strange behavior lately, all the questions she asked about Robert, finally made sense.

"How could you?" Abby shoved herself off the bed and paced around the room, fingers pressed to her temples. "I've been such a fool. When Robert rejected me I poured out my heart to you. And you were oh so supportive. All the time you dated him behind my back. That must have given you both a good laugh."

Emily shook her head. "No. It's not like that. By the time we hooked up, you were over him."

"Didn't it bother you how bad he hurt me? Me, the sister you're supposed to love so much."

"He didn't mean to hurt you. He just…"

Abby raked fingers through her hair. "Stop it! To think I actually trusted you…"

Emily sprang from the bed and laid a hand on

Abby's shoulder. "You *can* trust me. Please, Abby, don't do this."

Abby flinched and pulled away. "Don't, just…don't, okay?"

Her sister's hand dropped. "You don't know how bad I wanted to tell you. It killed me because I couldn't confide in you."

Abby blew out a breath through pursed lips. Did she want Abby to understand, to feel sorry for her? Not a chance. "Oh yeah, I can imagine how bad it's been, you poor misunderstood soul. Not easy to keep an affair all to yourself."

"It's not an affair, I swear. We're just dating, that's all."

"That's all? Just dating?" Abby shook her head. "First, I don't believe it because I know Robert. Second, just dating is supposed to make it less of a betrayal?"

"Okay. I won't see him anymore. I promise. I don't want you to hate me." Tears streamed down Emily's face and she sniffed. "I can't stand it if you stop loving me."

Any other time the tears would soften Abby. Not this time. This time Emily went too far. Fury burned through her as she glared at the woman she trusted with her life. She had to get out of here.

Abby stepped toward the door. Emily took a step too.

"No." Abby held a hand up, palm facing forward. "Right now you look like every woman Robert cheated with. I can't stand the sight of you." Abby bolted through the door and pushed her way into Carrie's room.

Carrie looked peaceful and innocent curled up in her sleeping bag. She prayed this sister would never betray her.

She pulled on the shorts and T-shirt she'd shed earlier. Anger simmered in her stomach, coming to a full boil. Tears stung her eyes as she threw clothes in her bag, and without a word she slipped out of the room, and left her parents' house.

***

The weekend did nothing to calm Abby's raging emotions. She sat at her desk Monday morning and tried to tamp down the jumbled images of Emily and Robert that swirled through her mind. No matter how hard she tried, the picture was imprinted on her brain. Her head ached and she felt sick to her stomach. She buried her face in her hands and a tear plopped through her fingers. Why would her sister betray her?

A tap at her door jerked her to attention. She grabbed a handful of tissues and tried to repair her face. "Come in."

Sam opened the door and stepped inside. A question formed in his eyes. He eased the door shut and walked to her desk. "You want to talk about it?"

She shrugged a shoulder. "Family problems."

The janitor slid into a chair, leaned back and laced his fingers on his lap. "I'm a good listener."

At his quiet comment, she looked at him and saw concern and compassion flick across his eyes. Fresh tears bit her eyes. She pulled in a long breath and words spilled from her in a torrent. The spoiled weekend, the confrontation with her sister, the betrayal, how hurt and angry she felt. She blew her nose and tossed the twentieth tissue in the trash.

"Then Mom calls me Saturday and tells me she doesn't see what the big deal is. She said Robert and I had been split up for six months before Emily started seeing him." She sniffed her nose. "Even my mother doesn't get it."

Empathy tightened Sam's voice. "I'm so sorry."

"Why can't people be honest?"

Sam furrowed his brow. He opened his mouth but before he could speak, his walkie-talkie crackled. "Sam, Mrs. Pringle needs to see you in her office."

"You need to take that."

He made no attempt to hide his irritation as he pulled the devise from his belt and pressed the button. "I'm on it," he said into the two-way, then shifted his gaze to Abby.

Abby smiled. "Go ahead, I'm okay, really."

"I've got to go." He shoved back his chair. "But I will be back. Can we do lunch?"

Abby nodded. "I'd like that."

***

Sam strode down the hall toward the assistant dean's office with Abby's words echoing in his ears. Why can't people just be honest? The comment stung. It was time to open up to her and tell her about his past and Sara before she found out from someone else.

He turned the corner and his thoughts slid away when he saw Sara outside Mrs. Pringle's office. She glared at him and said, "I'm supposed to tell you to go on in."

"What's this about?"

Sara shrugged. "Go find out."

Sam opened the door. Mrs. Pringle sat behind her desk.

"Have a seat, Mr. Ford."

Sam slid into a chair.

"I assume you saw Sara in the waiting area?"

Sam nodded.

"I've had quite a lengthy talk with her this morning." She tugged off her glasses and rubbed her eyes. "I know her mother's relocated, that's why I sent for you."

"Yes, Linda left this weekend."

Mrs. Pringle cleared her throat. "Sara failed the final in Algebra. That could pull her grade down substantially if she doesn't buckle down."

"She's always done so well in Algebra." Sam shook his head. "I don't understand."

"To be honest with you, I don't either. This is so unlike her." The assistant dean scooted his daughter's folder across the desk. "She has always been an A student. The past few weeks, her grades have slipped in all her classes."

Sam reached for the chart. He knew Sara was a good student and applied herself in all her studies, until recently. Until he made his confession and tore her heart out.

"Mr. Ford, if she does some extra credit, Professor Hughes says she can pull her Algebra grade back up to a B minus. He has already spoken with her and she's well aware of what she needs to do."

"I'll talk to her." Sam sighed, and wondered how he could get through to her.

"I felt you'd want to have a word with her. That's why I asked her to wait."

"I appreciate it."

"Thank you for coming in." Mrs. Pringle rose from her chair. "Parenting can be hard, I know. Hang in there."

Sam nodded, took a deep breath and went out to talk to his daughter. "What happened with your Algebra final, honey?"

Sara shrugged. "I was sick that day, couldn't concentrate."

"You've always been so good in math. Is there anything I can do to…"

"It's no big deal."

"It is a big deal when you flunk a final."

Sara popped up from the chair. "Well, if you don't want me to flunk history you'll cut this short and let me get back to class."

"Okay, go ahead, but we'll talk more about this later."

"There's nothing more to talk about," Sara said and stomped down the hall.

Sam watched her go, and wondered if she was headed for even more trouble. He was almost certain he'd smelled smoke on her clothes, but not sure enough to confront her.

***

Sam stopped at the Deli and picked up two sandwiches and a couple bottled waters before he met Abby for lunch. He figured she wouldn't have much of an appetite. He sure didn't.

They sat in relative silence as he drove the golf cart toward the small lake on campus. The oak trees gave way to a meadow bright with flowers, their round faces open toward the sun. Light glistened and seared off the crystal clear water. This area was secluded and serene. Just what they both needed he suspected.

Abby stepped from the cart and looked around. She pulled in a deep breath. "It's beautiful here."

Sam nodded. "It is." He grabbed the food and a blanket, then guided her to a spot a few feet from shore. He spread out the blanket and set the food down.

"Hope this is okay," he said.

"It's perfect." Abby sat, knees bent, her arms wrapped around her legs.

Sam eased onto the blanket and sat beside her. "Are you okay?"

"I'm fine now, really. Thanks for being there for me when I needed someone."

"Anytime."

He opened the bottled waters, handed one to Abby and took a long swallow from his.

"You were honest with me and I want to be honest with you. I need to talk to you, let you know who I really am."

A puzzled look rippled across her face. "You sound so serious."

"I am."

Now it was his turn for revelations. He started at the beginning and let his past unfold. Abby listened, nodding here and there, as he poured out the truth.

When he took a breath, Abby's eyes widened. "You're a doctor?"

"Yes, a pediatric oncologist."

"Then why in the world are you working as a janitor?"

"Two reasons. One, I wanted to be close to my daughter."

"Oh?"

"Abby," he said, his words slow, deliberate. "Sara Tennyson is my child."

"Sara?" Her eyes narrowed a fraction as she scrutinized him.

Sam nodded. "I had no idea her mother was pregnant when we broke up. She moved away and didn't tell me. Three years ago she called and told me I had a little girl."

"Oh, my gosh." Abby's eyes grew wide. "After all those years she suddenly decided to tell you?"

"Yeah. She said it was time to tell me because Sara had so many questions about her paternity."

"You didn't believe that?"

"At first, yes." He rubbed the side of his face. "Then later I figured it was because of the guy she married. She wanted time for him and didn't want to be saddled with the total responsibility of a kid anymore."

"Poor Sara."

Sam flinched. Yes, poor Sara. She's the one that had to muddle through childhood without her father, living with a mother who wouldn't put her child's needs ahead of her own.

"Sara begged me not to tell anyone I'm her father. She was embarrassed I took a janitor job. At the time I would do whatever I had to do to be a part of Sara's life. Then after I made a choice to accept the Lord into my heart, God started dealing with me about my deception."

Abby nodded. "I know what you mean. God's small voice can be pretty loud."

"Really loud," Sam said, as he remembered his struggle. "It kept tugging at my heart and though I didn't want to break my promise to Sara, I couldn't ignore it."

Abby looked at him, dipped her head in a nod.

"Two weeks ago, I confessed to Mrs. Pringle. Now Sara hates me, feels I can't be trusted." He took a long swallow of the water.

"I am so sorry, and I know it has to hurt, but give Sara some time. I'm sure she'll come around."

"I don't know…" Sam focused on his hand as he rubbed a thumb across his palm.

Abby opened her water, took a drink, then recapped the bottle.

"I told you I had two reasons for coming here." He raked unsteady fingers through his hair and lifted his head. "I couldn't deal with the dejection of watching kids die, being helpless to save them."

He recognized the empathy in her eyes, "That had to be hard on you." Her comment was quiet, gentle.

Sam's chest tightened, making it difficult to catch a breath. "Around the time I learned about Sara, I had a terminal patient, Cindy, a ten year old little girl. She fought a battle with pancreatic cancer. Right up to the very end. So did I, but no matter what combination of treatments I tried, she never responded. I watched her suffer and deteriorate to a skeleton in a matter of months. Believe me, she struggled through months of violent illness from the chemo. Bless her heart, there was never a day she couldn't muster a smile for me, she was so brave."

Sam stopped for a breath. Abby sat quietly, pinned him with an intent look and appeared to be deep in thought.

Sam slid a hand across his brow and continued. "It broke my heart the morning she died. Her mother and I were with her, both of us knew the end was near. I sat by her bedside all night, I talked to her and read to her. I don't know how much of what I said got through. But I'd like to believe she knew... well, knew I was there and loved her. At eleven minutes 'til six she died in my arms. I held her for a long time, just looking at the precious life that had been yanked away before she had the chance to live."

Abby picked up the water bottle and handed it to him. He took a drink, and then another, letting the cool liquid moisten his arid mouth.

"I thought of my daughter and how I'd missed out on her life and I knew I had to make my time with Sara count. I also knew I couldn't go through another Cindy and survive. It was too hard, hurt too much. I, Dr. Sam Ford, was the healer, yet I couldn't heal Cindy."

"Oh, Sam," Abby said, hardly above a whisper. A sheen of moisture clouded her eyes.

He blinked away the tears that threatened his own eyes. He opened his mouth to follow up with a comment to lighten the atmosphere, but the words died on his tongue when Abby reached out and laid a gentle hand on his arm and looked at him with what he read as emanating compassion.

They sat in silence and looked at the lake, the uneaten lunch in the bag beside them.

CHAPTER SEVEN

A thud outside her office resounded in Abby's ears. She pushed back from her desk and stepped across the floor. When she opened the door she saw two red-faced sophomore girls, Sara's buddies Brenda and Melissa, hurling not so kind remarks back and forth. When they spotted her they stopped mid-sentence.

"What's the problem? Abby asked.

"Her." Brenda pointed at her nemesis. "She yanked my cell phone out of my hand and threw it down." She pushed her blond hair off her forehead, stooped to pick up the phone. "It's a wonder she didn't break it." She opened her purse and tucked the cell inside. But she didn't get it zipped before Abby spied the pack of opened cigarettes in her bag.

"It's a picture of *my* boyfriend," Melissa shouted at the blonde.

"In your dreams," Brenda said, her voice an octave too high.

Abby gathered in a fortified breath. "Girls,

please, calm down."

"Talk to her. She's the one that needs to chill." The brunette shot Brenda a glare, then turned and huffed down the hall.

The blonde rubbed her hand gently over the outside of her purse. "He's not her boyfriend anymore Nurse Abby. They broke up a month ago, but she won't let go. She thinks she owns him."

"Is he your boyfriend now?"

Brenda's face brightened. "Sorta, he's taking me to the sophomore dance Friday night."

Abby patted the girl's arm and smiled. "Go on to class. I'll have a talk with Melissa later."

"Thanks, Nurse Abby." The girl pulled her purse strap over her shoulder and headed down the hall.

Abby shook her head, turned and spotted Clark standing in the doorway of the chemistry lab across the hall. He stepped over to Abby and grinned.

"Boy trouble?" Clark asked.

"Yeah." Abby watched Brenda turn the corner at the end of the corridor and slip out of sight. "I remember when I was that age. Life can get so complicated."

Clark nodded. He shifted his gaze to her eyes. "I stopped by to see if you'd like to join me for a coffee break."

Sam's face flashed across Abby's mind and she made a quick decision. "I don't think so, but thanks for asking."

"Okay, see you." He tipped his head, turned and walked away.

She returned to her desk, picked up a pen and pulled a chart toward her to scribble some notes.

She couldn't focus. Instead, she thought about Sam. How sad he'd looked when he poured out his heart to her yesterday. She admired his honesty. She wondered if there could be a future with him. She sent up a silent prayer, then refocused on the work in front of her.

Forty-five minutes later when she finished the last chart, she leaned back in her chair and rubbed the back of her neck.

"Hi."

Abby turned. Sam stood in the doorway, one shoulder against the doorframe and he smiled at her. His smile could stop her earth from rotating.

"Hi, come in."

"You looked so engrossed in your work. I didn't want to disturb you."

"You're not."

"Have you got time for a break?"

Abby rose from her desk. "Sure. I'd like that." She fell into step with him as they headed toward the dining hall.

"About yesterday," he said. "I hope I didn't throw too much at you."

She shook her head. "No, not at all. I'm glad you shared your past with me."

"I wanted you to know, especially about Sara." She watched sadness cloud his face.

"Things will work out. Sara's a levelheaded kid. She's upset right now, but I'm sure she loves her dad."

"I hope you're right."

"Like I said, just give her some time. She'll come around."

Sam nodded. He stopped outside the cafeteria and turned toward her. "How are you holding up? I know you're struggling with family issues yourself."

"I'm okay. I still find it hard to believe Emily would do something like this to me."

"And you resent her." It was more of a statement than a question.

"Do you blame me?"

"No. But maybe she didn't realize you'd be so hurt. Maybe she's truly sorry."

Abby shrugged. She mulled over his remark. As mad and hurt as she was at Emily, she missed her sister like crazy. She missed the closeness they'd always shared. But Emily betrayed her in the worst possible way and she didn't know how to deal with it. The thought of Emily and Robert together nauseated her.

Sam opened the door and they stepped into the dining hall and got coffee. Sam nudged Abby to a table and they sat down.

Five minutes later Florence set a tray loaded with bagels and cream cheese on the table and gave Sam a wide grin. "And don't tell me you're not hungry."

Sam tossed the cook a wink, stood and pulled out a chair adjacent to him.

Florence plopped into the seat. She reached over, brushed a strand of hair from Sam's forehead and smiled. "You need a haircut."

"Yeah?" Sam cocked his head to the side and gave Florence a mischievous look. "Who says so?"

"I say so. And you can't argue with your elders."

He chuckled and rubbed two knuckles under

Florence's chin. "I'd never try to argue with you."

Florence harrumphed, her gaze shifting between Sam and Abby. "You know, you two make a nice looking couple." She leaned back in her chair and crossed her arms over her chest. "Yes, real nice."

Heat rushed up Abby's neck. She took a sip from her mug to hide her embarrassment. If the remark alluding to them as a couple bothered Sam, he didn't let on as the light banter continued. It was impossible for Abby to miss the endearing bond between Sam and the cook. Florence doted on him and he ate it up.

"I hate to leave such good company but I've got to get back to work." Florence pushed back from the table. She took two steps, stopped and swayed a little.

Sam jumped from his seat, put his arm around the cook and directed her back to the table. "Are you okay?"

"I'm fine." Florence looked at Abby and shook her head. "It's nothing."

Abby aimed a finger at her. "You're having another dizzy spell, aren't you?"

"Another?" Sam's voice spiked. "You mean this has happened before?"

Florence scowled. "What's so bad about a little dizzy spell?"

"It's not normal," Abby said.

"She's right." Sam took Florence's wrist and placed two fingers over the radial pulse. "One twenty, that's too fast."

Abby nodded.

"Come on." Sam rose from his chair, helped

Florence to her feet.

"Where?" Florence asked.

"To Abby's office so we can check your blood pressure."

"We? What are you now, Sam, a doctor?"

Abby and Sam shared a look.

"What?" The cook's eyes darted from one of them to the other.

"I'll tell you later," Sam said. "First, I'm getting you to the infirmary."

Florence frowned. "Okay, I'll go. But I'm telling you I'm fine."

They gathered Florence between them and walked the few feet to the nurse's office. Abby guided her to a chair, then wrapped a blood pressure cuff around her arm.

"180 over 110." Abby unwound the cuff and laid it down. "Way too high."

Sam nodded then looked at the older woman. "You're going to the doctor."

"I don't have time. I've got work to do. Do you want me to get fired?"

"You're not going to get fired." He put a hand on Florence's elbow to help her stand and then slipped his arm around her shoulder. "Come on, I'll drive you."

"You worry too much," Florence said.

"So sue me."

Florence pulled a palm across her brow. "Really, Sam, I don't think I need …"

"Yes you do," he said.

Abby gave the reluctant lady a pat. "He's right. You need to get checked out."

"Harrump." The cook shot a look at Sam. "At least she's a nurse. Maybe I'll pay attention to her."

Sam gave her a gentle nudge toward the door. "That's right, sweetie. You listen to Abby."

Abby walked with Sam and Florence to the back entrance and waited beside Florence while Sam pulled his Lexus up to the door.

Sam hopped out of the car and helped Florence get in. He turned and winked at Abby. "She's in good hands."

"I don't doubt that." Abby smiled and watched until the car was out of sight before she headed back to her office. She hummed to herself, warmth radiated through her body. There was much more to admire about Sam than she had originally thought.

A future with Sam? Might just be possible, Abby mused.

* * *

Saturday morning, Sam arrived at the stables early. He had Hero and Savannah saddled and ready to go by the time Abby got there. She looked stunning this morning. But she always looked good to him.

"Hi, Sam." The light sparkled off her white teeth when she smiled.

Sam scanned her face and lingered on her green eyes. He could get lost in that deep emerald sea. "Hi, yourself."

Abby rubbed Hero's muzzle. "I see the horses are ready."

"Yep. And I think you're ready to handle the

riding trail today."

"You're the teacher." He could see the mischief in her eyes. "And a mighty fine one, I might add."

"Why thank you." He bowed. "If I didn't know better, I'd think you were trying to score points with your instructor. Such a shame."

Abby slapped her forehead with the heel of her hand. "Forgive me. I must have lost my head for a minute."

"Just so you don't make a habit of it."

Abby's lips curved up at the corners as she untied Hero and mounted the gelding. She sat in the saddle, shoulders back yet relaxed, as if she'd been born to do exactly that. You would never know she hadn't been on a horse until a few weeks ago.

With one foot in the stirrup, Sam swung his leg up and over. "Follow me." He winked, reined Savannah around and rode through the gate past the pen and onto the trail. He glanced over his shoulder. "You with me?"

"Uh huh. Right behind you."

Her voice was steady. Not choppy like the first day when she'd bounced around in the saddle. She'd come a long way in a fairly short time.

The trail widened and Sam eased Savannah to a stop and waited until Abby was beside him. She was close enough he could reach out and take her hand, but he didn't.

When she glanced toward him, his breath caught in his throat. His awareness of her was an almost tangible thing, disconcerting in its intensity. He'd never felt like this before. He needed to figure out how this woman managed to infiltrate his soul in such a short time.

He pressed his heels gently against his horse's side and she moved forward. "I stopped by and checked on Florence this morning."

"Oh, yeah. How's she doing?"

"Great, spunky as ever. She'll be back to work on Monday."

"I'm sure that makes her happy."

Sam laughed. "Oh, yeah. She's not one to just sit around idle."

"I'm glad you convinced her to seek medical help."

He nodded. "She's like a second mom to me. And I sure don't want to lose her."

"How's she doing with her meds?"

"More compliant than I thought she'd be." He shook his head. "You know how headstrong that woman is."

"I think this episode scared her enough she'll do what the doctor says."

Sam nodded. "She has to deal with both hypertension *and* hypothyroidism. No wonder she's been so tired."

"Did you ever tell her you are a physician?"

"Yeah. But I don't know if she believed me. She just thinks I'm grandiose."

Abby laughed. "I'm sure she believes you. She knows you wouldn't lie to her."

After a pleasant hour on the trail, Sam headed Savannah toward the stables. "I hope you're hungry. I packed enough food to feed an army."

"I'm starved. Riding really works up an appetite."

A few minutes later, they dismounted and led the horses through the gate. After Sam unsaddled the horses they snickered and made their way to the water trough.

He guided Abby through the gate, stopped and leaned against the fence. "Have you talked to your sister?"

Abby shook her head. "No, she's called a couple of times, but I never pick up. I don't have anything to say to her right now."

"Does she leave a message?"

"Yeah, I ignore it." Abby sighed, shifted her feet. "I know I'm going to have to get over this and forgive her. But right now I'm just too angry."

"It's hard, isn't it?"

Abby nodded.

Just then, Sam caught sight of some kids hanging around the training pen. He looked closer. It was Sara, with Brenda Arlington and two other girls. Shivers catapulted up his spine. These girls had questionable reputations and he didn't like his daughter hanging around with such a rough crowd.

She looked toward him and quickly turned away. She said something to the girls and her friends headed toward the parking lot.

Sam shot a look at Abby as she eyed the group. "Do you know those girls with Sara?"

"I do. But not very well." He saw a strange look cloud her features. He wondered if she knew more about Sara's friends than she wanted to admit.

"I'll be right back. I'm going to speak to that girl. Then we can head to the lake."

"Okay. Take your time."

Sam walked the few feet to his daughter. Sara, as predicted, had a scowl on her face.

"Hi, honey. What are you doing here?" Sam asked.

"I might ask you the same thing." Sara tossed a look toward Abby. "Why are you hanging around with *her*?"

"Giving her a riding lesson." Why couldn't Sara at least try to be civil?

"Why would you do that?"

"Why not? She wanted to learn to ride."

"Sure I bet." Sara drew her arms tight across her chest. "Does she know you're a doctor?"

"What's wrong with you, Sara? Abby is a nice lady."

"She knows, doesn't she? About me? That's so disgusting. I swear if my friends find out I'll… I'll…"

"You'll what? Hate me? I think you already do a pretty good job of that."

"At least you've got something straight."

Sam lost patience; he'd had it with her belligerence. "Sara," he said his words slow, deliberate, firm. "You can hate me all you want, I can't stop you. But I am your father, and you will show me some respect."

Sara's lips settled into a thin, unyielding line and she glared at him. "Yes. Sir." She flung the words at him, then turned and sprinted toward the school.

Sam pulled in a slow, calming breath, held it a beat, and blew it out. He wasn't going to let Sara's bad attitude spoil his picnic with Abby. He turned and strode back to the barn lot.

Abby looked at him. "Didn't go well, I take it?"

"Not well at all." Sam raked a hand through his hair and shook his head. "Thank goodness I only have one kid to deal with. I sure couldn't handle another."

CHAPTER EIGHT

A blanket of sadness wrapped around Abby as she watched the handsome janitor pull a cooler from the trunk and slide it in the back of the golf cart. He slipped behind the wheel and shot Abby a wink. "Let's eat."

She smiled and tried to hide the disappointment from his earlier remark. His words—*thank goodness I only have one kid*—cut across her heart like only the truth could do. Those words proved there could be no future between them.

They stopped near the bank of Brighton's lake and Sam said, "I have fried chicken and potato salad." He tossed a blanket to Abby.

"Where'd you get it, KFC?" She spread the cover out on the grass and reached for the plastic containers as Sam gathered them from the cooler.

He tilted his head to the side and gave her a half grin. "I made it."

"You cook?" Yet another revelation from this man that seemed to be full of surprises.

"Yep. Being a bachelor all these years, I had to learn how to cook or eat every meal out. And that gets old really fast."

"I can relate to that." Abby arranged the containers on the blanket and opened them.

She took a sip of the iced tea he produced from the cooler, already in a bottle so it was easy for her to drink.

"Oh my goodness, Sam, this is really good. I'm impressed," she said as she chewed on a chicken leg.

He smiled. "I am a pretty good chicken-fryer, if I do say so myself."

Abby leaned back on one arm and stole a glance at him as he shoveled in a bite of potato salad. She liked this man. There was no doubt about it. He was a good, honest man, a Christian. But he'd made it abundantly clear how he felt about more children.

Sadness tugged at Abby's heart. She wanted a child. She yearned to experience carrying her own baby, and she was running out of time. At thirty-five, her biological clock ticked away. Why, when she'd found such a great guy, did she have to give up hopes of a future with him?

"Penny for your thoughts." Sam interrupted her reverie. "Are you okay?"

She smiled. "Just thinking what a nice man you are."

A red glow settled over his features. "I'm flattered." He tucked the leftover chicken into the cooler, and adjusted his position so he looked directly into her eyes. "Abby, you're different from any woman I've ever met. I'm so thankful the Lord brought you into my life."

The huskiness in his voice tightened her throat, and she had to swallow before she could respond. "We never know what our future holds."

"No, we don't."

His gaze held hers until she looked away. She cleared her throat and steered to safer ground. "Does Florence know you can cook?"

His eyes narrowed a bit at her sudden subject change, but he had a quick response. "No. Florence thinks I'm helpless."

"I'll never tell. Your secret is safe with me."

Sam chuckled, the sound a pleasant rumble in his chest. He reached inside the cooler. "Dessert?"

"Sure. What is it?"

He pulled out a plastic container and popped off the cover. "Apple pie, hope you like it."

"If you tell me you baked this, I'm outta here." Abby lifted a brow and raked a slice onto her plate.

"I'm afraid not, compliments of a little bakery down the street from me."

Abby slid a forkful of pie into her mouth. She glanced at Sam and wondered how she would ever find the strength to walk away. She loved sitting beside him, talking and laughing with him, it felt so right. She could easily toss her needs aside and give in to her attraction to this generous guy that was the epitome of a great man. She swallowed a lump in her throat and sighed as she remembered the fiasco with Robert. For seven years she compromised her beliefs and goals for a man. Abby wasn't willing to do that again. Better to stop seeing Sam now than compromise her dreams.

* * *

Late Monday afternoon, Abby wiped the counter in the infirmary with antibacterial solution, then washed her hands. She stepped into her office and nearly collided with the history professor.

"Hi, Clark."

He smiled. "Hi, did you have a busy day?"

Abby nodded. "Very busy." She slid her purse over her shoulder.

Clark shifted his weight from one foot to the other. "How about a mocha at the deli before you head home?"

Abby looked at the professor. Why not? Maybe it would take her mind off Sam. "That sounds great."

Clark's eyes crinkled at the corners as a wide smile spread across his face. He opened the door, and she stepped across the threshold. Abby walked beside him to the deli and they ordered drinks. They sat at a small table overlooking the atrium.

"They make the best mochas I've ever tasted," Clark said as the young waitress set the mugs on the table.

Abby picked up her cup, blew on the steaming liquid then took a sip. "Mmmm. Your're right."

Clark traced a circle around the rim of his mug. "I hear you're going to be one of the chaperones for the freshmen girls' camping trip."

Abby nodded. "Uh huh."

"Have you ever been to Fort DeSota Park?"

"No. Have you?"

"Yeah, a couple of times. It's a nice place. You'll like it."

"Hmmm." Abby idly tapped the spoon on the side of her cup, mentally packing for the outing. Sam would be the other chaperone. She had bitter-sweet feelings about spending so much time with him. How could she be with him the entire weekend and still guard her already muddled heart?

"How are the riding lessons coming along?" Clark's words brought her back to the present.

"Really well. Sam's great with horses. He's taught me a lot."

"Oh, yeah?" She recognized resentment as it flickered across Clark's face. He turned the subject into an elaborate explanation about a not so positive riding experience he had as a teenager. His vivid description made her chuckle.

"So, I've steered clear of equine since my youth." Clark ended his fifteen minute reverie with a laugh.

"You know what they say, when you fall off you need to get right back on."

He shook his head. "Oh no, not me. I'm quite happy to stay on the ground."

Abby smiled and picked up her cup and swallowed down the last of the creamy chocolate. "Thanks for the coffee." She scooted her chair back. "I enjoyed it."

"I'll walk out with you."

As they strolled across the parking lot, Clark shared another amusing story and made Abby laugh. He opened her car door and waited while she slid in and said goodnight.

"Have a nice evening," he said as he turned and walked away.

She slipped the key in the ignition and glanced in her rearview mirror. Florence strode across the parking lot, head bent low. Abby pressed the button and the window slid down. "Hey Florence. How are you doing?"

Florence didn't look up. "I'm okay." She pulled open the door on an Escort and got inside.

Abby slipped the car into reverse. She wondered why the cook was in such a bad mood.

* * *

"Hey, Sam." Florence poked her head in the utility room Friday morning.

"Hi, yourself," he said as he pulled tan paint from the shelf and set the can on his cart. "How's my favorite lady?"

"I'm good." The cook stepped to the cart, ran a finger over the top of the paint lid. "You gonna do some painting today?"

"Yeah, touch-ups in the library."

"When you get done, come by the kitchen. I've got something for you."

"What's that?"

"A raspberry cake, with gobs of milk chocolate icing."

He cocked his head to the side. "Why do you want me to be fat?"

She laughed. "You, Sam, will never be fat."

Florence walked around the cart and stood next to him. "Are you ready to play chaperone this

105

weekend?"

"Yep. We're leaving right after school."

"Abby going too?"

Sam nodded. Florence gave him a fleeting look but remained silent. "Something on your mind today, Florence?"

"Yes, as a matter of fact there is." She took in a deep breath and blew it out. "I saw Abby with that history professor."

"And?"

"And they were pretty cozy, if you know what I mean."

Sam searched her face. "If you have a point, I wish you'd make it."

"Well, I hate to be the one to burst your bubble, but they had coffee together in the cafeteria more than once. Right under my nose, mind you. Then last night I caught them coming out of the deli. They had their heads together and laughed and joked all the way to her car."

Sam struggled to maintain a neutral expression. "They're friends," he said and tried to make his voice sound more unconcerned than he felt.

"Well, they looked mighty chummy to me." Florence laid a hand on Sam's shoulder. "Call me a nosey, old woman, Sam. But I'm worried about you. I don't want to see you get hurt."

"Florence, you're sweet to worry about me. But don't. Abby is the kindest…"

"I'm telling you, that nurse is trouble." Tears glistened on her eyelashes and she shook her head. "You're a good man and you deserve someone who'll appreciate you. Not someone who's playing with your emotions."

Sam gave his elderly friend a hug, stepped back and held her at arm's length. "Abby's not a bad person. She wouldn't deliberately hurt anyone. And we aren't exactly a couple. She can see anyone she wants."

"Ha! I bet she never even gave you a second glance until she knew you were an important doctor."

"You're wrong about her. I promise you, Abby's not like that."

"Well, don't say I didn't warn you when she dumps you for that professor." Florence squeezed his hands. "I've got to get back to work. Stop in for that cake later."

Sam nodded. "I will."

She turned and headed down the hall.

"You might be a nosey, old woman but you're well-meaning and I love you. I hope you know that," Sam called to Florence.

She tossed him a grin over her shoulder and continued down the corridor.

Sam wheeled his cart over the threshold and pondered Florence's words. Despite his bravado, his heart took a massive kick when Florence described Abby with Clark. He wondered if he'd read more into their friendship than Abby felt.

* * *

A buzz of anticipation permeated the school van as David, the driver, pulled out of Brighton. Sara sat in the back with her friends. She was sullen, and shot razor-sharp looks in Sam and Abby's direction.

Sam shifted his weight in the seat and looked at Abby. "Sara's not happy I'm one of the chaperones."

"She'll lighten up once we get to the park." He heard the empathy in her voice.

He shrugged and closed his eyes to remember a time when Sara had been happy to be with him. Two years ago when he flew to Tampa to spend the weekend with his daughter, they spent an entire Saturday exploring De Sota Park.

The park, in Pinellas County, consisted of several interconnected islands. It was located on the southern-most tip of land south of St. Petersburg. After a morning on the recreation trail that meandered from one end of the park to the other, they walked the beach, nibbled on hot dogs and let the gentle waves caress their feet. What a happy day! One of few he'd had with his daughter.

Sam opened his eyes. Abby peered out the window as they sped down I-275. He sat shoulder to shoulder with her and inhaled her fresh distinctive scent, something fruity that made his heart do a flip.

She turned toward him. "Is Florence okay?"

"She's doing great."

"She acted strange when I saw her earlier this week. She barely spoke to me."

"She probably was a little preoccupied." Florence hadn't mentioned she'd shunned Abby. If she would give Abby a chance she would find out what a wonderful person she was.

An hour later, the driver pulled the van through the entrance of Fort De Sota Park. David turned right and headed down the main thoroughfare toward the camping section at the southern end. He parked between two cabbage palm trees.

It took Sam, Abby and David forty-five minutes to get the vehicle unloaded and the tents set up, one for Abby and the girls, another smaller one for Sam. David said his farewells and promised to return Sunday morning at ten o'clock.

Sam and Abby headed down the well-kept palm lined path to where the girls gathered in the shaded waterfront picnic area a hundred feet from the campsite. Several wooden picnic tables were spaced around a large central pavilion overlooking the Skyway Bridge that spanned Tampa Bay. A few of the tables were occupied by other campers.

"We better grab a table before they fill up," Abby said.

"Yeah, I'm starved," Brenda said and headed to the nearest table. "What's for dinner?"

"Florence packed a big cooler for us, so I'm sure it's good," Sam said. He hoped she'd thrown in some raspberry cake. "Who wants to help me tote the cooler?"

Three girls volunteered. Sara wasn't one of them, but Sam wasn't surprised. He figured she'd keep her distance this weekend.

After dinner and clean up, Sam and Abby and the girls explored the camp. He wondered if Sara remembered the nice time they spent here when she was twelve. If she did, she didn't let on. She remained silent and sullen as they padded across the park.

Before they headed back to the camp site over an

hour later, they stopped at a concession stand on the pier and Sam treated everyone to big bags of popcorn, buttered of course.

* * *

Late the next afternoon, Sam and Abby bought lemonade at the same stand near the bay side pier. They found a bench that allowed them to look down at the girls and watch as they frolicked on the beach. Rollerbladers and bikers passed in front of them. On the powder white sand, kids threw Frisbees. The pier buzzed with tourists.

Abby's phone buzzed and she slid it from her bag, looked at it and shook her head. She slipped it back in the bag.

Sam gave her a puzzled look.

Abby met his gaze and shrugged. "Emily."

"Oh."

"I don't want to deal with her right now and ruin the weekend."

"Still trying to sort through things?"

"Yeah." Abby shrugged. "She said she and Robert are just friends, nothing serious. She even promised not to see him anymore."

"Maybe that's true."

"Maybe, but I need to get my head on straight before I talk to her. I don't want to end up saying something I'll regret."

Sam looked at her and wondered how long it would take before she worked through the problems with her sister. It bothered her and he knew from experience it wouldn't help to ignore it.

"The girls are having a great time." Abby changed the subject and he didn't press the issue. She leaned closer and looked at the beach below, her breath warm on his ear, her hair like silk brushed against his jaw. "Oh, look. Olivia has found a sand dollar."

Sam smiled and did his best to focus in the direction she nodded. He wanted the superb day with his pretty lady to never end. It was unparalleled. After breakfast, they took an extended walk on the hiking trail, stopped for lunch at Don CeSars, and ended up on the pier.

"Not only have the girls had a great time, I have too. It's been nice having this time with you," he said.

Abby pulled in a slow breath and studied him. Then she nodded and said, "It has been perfect, hasn't it?"

Sam sat close to Abby on the bench. A combination of sea air and Abby's scent wafted over him and turned his insides to jelly. He wanted to put his arm around her, to pull her to him and kiss her. He was close to doing it, so close his stomach clenched like it was being squeezed in a vice. He swallowed down a dry throat and said, "Yes, perfect."

The afternoon turned to evening and the girls bought hot dogs then joined Sam and Abby on the pier for a little people watching and a lot of chatter. Ready to call it a day, they all hustled back to the campsite for a marshmallow roast.

By eleven o'clock everyone was stifling yawns. Abby and the girls headed for their tent and Sam sacked out in his smaller tent. He couldn't get his mind off Abby. He turned on his side, tucked the edge of the sleeping bag under his chin and fell asleep.

The next thing Sam knew, a voice called his name. Abby's voice.

He scrambled from the cot and looked at his watch. It was midnight. He pulled on his shorts and slipped a T-shirt over his head. "What's wrong?"

"Sara, Brenda and Melissa are gone."

"Gone? What do you mean, gone?" He tried to shake the sleep induced fog from his brain.

"They're not in the tent. A noise woke me and I got up to investigate. I found their cots empty."

Sam raked a hand through his disheveled hair. "Hold on a minute." He slipped into his tent, grabbed a flashlight and stepped back outside. He flipped the light on and Abby walked beside him as they started down the trail.

Whispers of teenage giggles drifted through the night air and Sam headed toward the sound.

On the far side of the small history museum, Sara and her friends sat at a picnic table with two teenage boys who looked to be at least seventeen.

Sam's jaw sagged open, but no words came.

"Girl's, get back to the tent," Abby said. "Now."

Surprise at Abby's angry tone flicked across the girls' faces. They got up and bustled down the trail.

Sam glared at the young men, then turned and hurried after his daughter. He caught up to Sara at the front of the tent. He grabbed her arm. "Just a minute, young lady."

Sara looked down at his grip, then looked at him.

"We were just talking. Nothing happened. It was no big deal."

"You sneaked out. That's a big deal. You're fourteen, too young for those boys. It is a big deal. Not only are you in trouble with me, you're in big trouble with the school."

"I swear we were just talking."

Sam's jaw jutted forward. "You just don't get it do you?"

Sara scuffed her foot back and forth on the ground.

"Go on. Get in there and get to bed. But this isn't over."

Sara shot him a look and pushed through the flap into the tent.

He walked to a nearby picnic table and slumped down on the bench. He put his head in his hands. Later, he felt a gentle touch on his shoulder and looked up.

"I've got the girls settled down." Abby slid onto the seat across from him.

He looked at her and shook his head. "What am I going to do with that girl?"

Abby sighed. "I wish I had an answer for you, but I don't." She bowed her head. "Let's pray."

Sam nodded and bowed his head too. Abby led in a short but heartfelt prayer asking for guidance and direction. Then she sat with him in silence for a few minutes.

"Why don't you try to get some sleep?" Abby suggested, and pulled herself up. "We'll be leaving before noon tomorrow."

Sam shuffled off the bench. He knew he'd never

be able to fall asleep, but he didn't want to keep Abby up all night. He could worry in his tent just as well as here.

CHAPTER NINE

"Good morning." Clark stepped to Abby's workstation first thing Tuesday morning and settled a hip on her desk. "Are you going to the tryouts for the senior drama production?"

She shook her head. "No, I'm afraid I can't. I'm booked all morning."

Sara, her first appointment was scheduled for eight o'clock and would be here soon. Abby was filled with more than a little apprehension. She hadn't seen Sara since the camping incident, and dreaded a confrontation with Sam's daughter.

"Bummer," Clark said. "I hoped we could go together."

Abby heard a muffled sound and turned. Sara stood in the doorway. She wore tight low ride jeans that hugged her petite frame and a pastel pink shirt that rested on her waistband. Abby caught a glimpse of bright pink toenails that peeked through her open-toed leather sandals.

"Am I interrupting something?" Sara's gaze

flicked back and forth between Abby and Clark, a smirk creased her face.

"Not at all." Clark straightened, shoved his hands in his pockets and moved toward the door. "I'll see you later."

Abby gave Clark a nod and turned toward the girl. "Come in, Sara, and have a seat." She motioned to a chair beside her desk.

The tips of her sleek, strappy lattice sandals showed beneath her jeans.

Abby pulled the chair up so her legs rested under the desk. She stared at Sara. She looked so much like her father with her dark wavy hair. Her lips were full and accentuated a dimple on her left cheek. She had Sam's eyes. They were wide set and a vivid blue. They were framed with thick dark lashes like her father's. They were both gorgeous people.

"How can I help you?" Abby asked.

"I need to get started on birth control. I think I'd prefer pills over the shot. I definitely don't want a patch."

Shocked, Abby struggled to maintain a neutral expression. "Have you been on birth control before?"

"Nope. But I think it's time, don't you?"

Sara's voice was sharp and unfriendly. It set Abby on edge. Was the girl wanting to goad her to say something she could take to her dad and try to hammer a wedge between them? "No. At your age, Sara, I'd opt for abstinence as the ideal form of birth control."

Sara's face turned pink. "Well, it's not your

choice, is it?"

Abby shrugged. "You asked."

"I've changed my mind. I don't want your advice. Just hook me up with some birth control."

A few silent seconds ticked by as Abby reflected on the situation, praying for wisdom. She could picture the devastated look on Sam's face if he heard his daughter's request.

Sara tapped two fingers on her lap and spoke again. "Well, how about the pills? When can I get them?"

"Sara, before I can just hand you a pack of birth control pills, I'll need to take a history and…"

Sara sneered. "You don't need a history. I'm sure my dad has filled you in on all the details of my past."

"I'm talking about a medical history." Abby opened her drawer and pulled out the appropriate form and laid it on the top of her desk.

Sara glared at Abby. "I bet it kills you that you can't tell my dad about this. But you can't, you know."

Abby's face burned. Why was Sara being such a jerk? "I'm very much aware of the confidentiality laws and I would never compromise them."

Sara shrugged. "I bet you hate it though. You'd love to tell Sam all about this visit, like he blabbed about me." She leaned back in her chair, drew her brows together and glowered at Abby. "I don't like to be laughed at."

"No one is laughing at you." She took a breath and chose her words carefully. "Your dad loves you very much. All he wants is to be a part of your life."

"How would you know what my dad wants? You barely know him."

"I've known him long enough to know how much he cares about you. I hear it in his voice when he talks about you and in his eyes when he sees you."

"Don't give me that. You only know what he tells you. If he cared about me so much he wouldn't have waited until I was nearly grown to show up in my life."

Abby sighed. Sam had no choice, but it wasn't her place to explain this to his daughter. "If you would give him half a chance, I'm sure he could clear up all your questions."

Sara's face clouded with resentment. "What makes you think I have any questions? I was fine before he started nosing around in my life and ruined everything." She shifted her weight in the chair and met Abby's gaze. "I wish he'd stayed in Chicago and left me alone."

"Your father is a good man, Sara. And he certainly doesn't need me to justify his actions."

"Yeah, right." Sara snorted and rolled her eyes. "The only reason you want my dad is because he's a doctor. You wouldn't have given a measly janitor the time of day."

The child was out of line and this was none of her business. Abby had half a mind to tell this belligerent girl just that. But she bit back sarcasm and said, "I'm sure you're not here to discuss my personal life. Let's get back to the birth control issue, shall we?"

"It's not an issue. I want the pill, simple as that."

She glared at Abby as if she dared her to come back with a counter.

Abby pressed her lips together. "Okay, Sara. Let's go over your history-*medical* history-and then I'll make an appointment for your exam with a nurse practitioner. Once I get a prescription from her I can give you the contraceptives."

The color drained from Sara's face and her lips turned white and tense. She gave the nurse a stare. Sara would soon learn, not everything in life happened as quickly as you'd like.

It took twenty minutes for her to drag the information she needed from her reluctant patient. When she finished, the girl pranced to the door with a smirk on her face. She turned to Abby, grinned and said, "Remember you can't tell Sam our little secret."

Abby's spirits dropped as she watched Sara leave. She paced back and forth between her desk and the doorway, while she fought with her conscience. She had information that Sam deserved to know. He was worried about his daughter and he, as her father, had the right to know what Sara planned to do. She wished she could talk to him about it; but, like it or not, she was bound by law to hold her tongue.

* * *

"You and that nurse are sure tight," Sara said as Sam held the car door for her after school Friday. "Are you two sleeping together? If so, be sure you use protection. You wouldn't want another little accident."

Sam braced himself and waited for his daughter to climb into the seat. He would not let her cocky attitude ruin the weekend. She barely acknowledged Abby in the atrium. Sara's 'hello' was rude at best. This kind of vibe was one he often picked up from his flippant daughter. "Nothing is going on."

"Sure, whatever."

"I've got tickets for Sea World tomorrow." He shut the door before she could argue with that. She loved Sea World; at least she had two years ago.

Sam circled to the driver's side and slid into the seat. He hoped she would meet him partway this weekend. He didn't ask for anything as earthshaking as halfway. If Sara would take a few steps in his direction, there might be enough common ground to sustain his hope she would forgive him even though he told everyone she was his daughter.

He pulled out of the parking lot and headed home. A few minutes later at his condo, Sara slipped out of her backpack and lowered herself into the recliner across from him.

"How about I order pizza and then we can watch a movie?"

Sara shrugged. "Whatever."

After he called Pizza Hut, he hung up and looked at her. He watched her as she thumbed through the DVD's. His were mostly the classics but earlier this week he stopped at a video store and asked a young man to recommend a couple movies a fourteen year old girl might enjoy.

To Sam's surprise the movie she picked wasn't

one of the new ones but *The White Cliffs of Dover* with Alan Marshall and Van Johnson. "That's one of my all-time favorites," he said.

"Oh yeah? I haven't seen it. But the blurb sounded good."

"Let's wait to start it until the pizza gets here."

She shrugged and plopped into her seat.

"Okay," he said and cleared his throat. "Let's talk a minute about what happened at the park last weekend. Now that we both have calmed down, we can discuss it without arguing. And believe me I don't want to argue with you this weekend, deal?"

"Fine with me." She frowned at him . "Mrs. Pringle gave me a week's detention, which I didn't think was fair, but you already know that."

Sam nodded. "I just want to make sure you understand why Abby and I were upset."

She shook her head. "Don't bring *her* into this. It's not her problem."

Sam hesitated and gave his daughter a puzzled look.

Sara narrowed her eyes. "It's just between us Sam. Let's keep it that way."

"Okay. Just between you and me, you know you can't traipse off to meet strangers…"

"They weren't strangers. Brenda, Melissa and I talked to them all afternoon at the beach. And we didn't go off to meet them. We were just walking around and ran into them. We didn't think we were doing anything wrong."

"You should never have left the tent without telling Abby."

"If we'd asked, she would've said no."

"I'm sure she would have." He pulled his eyebrows together. "Sara, it was midnight."

"Okay, okay. Maybe it was a dumb thing to do."

"I hope you realize what an unwise choice you made. If Abby hadn't woke up and something bad happened to you girls, we wouldn't have known about it until the next morning."

Sara huffed. "I know. I won't pull something that lame again."

"I'm glad to hear that. Now let's concentrate on having a good weekend. Does Sea World sound like fun?"

Sara shrugged, flipped on the TV and turned the volume down. "Tell me something, Sam. Why did it take you twelve years to finally contact me?"

He looked at his daughter, the taste of regret sharp on his tongue. "I didn't have a choice. I didn't know about you until two years ago."

"Yeah. Like I'm gonna buy that."

"It's the truth. I didn't have a clue."

"And I suppose you never even knew Mom was pregnant?"

"I had no idea. Believe me, if I'd known I would have been there for both of you."

Sara twirled a strand of long hair around her right index finger and met Sam's gaze. "I wonder why Mom didn't tell you?"

Sam shrugged. "I don't know. I've asked myself that many times."

Sara kicked off her sandals, then tucked her feet under her. "What was your reaction when Mom told you about me?" He could see the doubt flash across her face as she tried to bait him.

Sam smiled as he conjured up the day nearly three years ago. "Total shock at first. I couldn't believe I was a father. Then after the news sank in, I was elated. Then scared to death. The realization that I had a daughter overwhelmed me. But believe me, I couldn't wait to meet my little girl."

"Really?" Her eyes widened and she tilted her head to the side.

"Yes, really. You're important to me. From the minute I became aware of you, I loved you. I hope you know that."

Sara's eyes narrowed and twin furrows dented her brow. He wished she'd let her defenses down and give him a break.

Their conversation was interrupted by the ring of the doorbell. "Our dinner," he said as he opened the door. The aroma from the hot pizza wafted over him and made his stomach growl.

Sara got paper plates and two sodas from the kitchen and set them on the coffee table. Once they both had a piece of pizza, Sara asked, "Do you think Mom's sorry she kept me a secret for so long?"

Sam shrugged and made a controlled effort to keep his voice calm. "That, I couldn't tell you."

"I wish I would have known you when I was little. I felt like an outsider around my friends. They always had a father around fussing over them. I was so jealous. I wanted a father. But I thought my father just didn't give a hoot."

"I'm so sorry you had to go through that." He closed his eyes and shook his head.

"I guess it's not really your fault." Sara shrugged. "But I'm sure Mom had her reasons for doing what she did."

He wondered what good could possibly come from keeping a father and daughter apart. He had questions on the tip of his tongue, but he bit them back. Sara wouldn't have any more answers than he did.

"Do you ever think about how different things could have been? You know, if you'd been around when I was a baby?"

"Yes. Every single day."

Just then, Sara's phone rang. He watched when she shifted her weight to one hip, pulled the cell from her pocket and looked at the ID. "Hey, Mom," she said.

Sam sighed. Linda had a knack for interruptions, and at the most inopportune times. Why had she called now? Right when Sara started to open up.

Sam walked into the kitchen to give his daughter some privacy. He leaned against the counter, raked his fingers through his hair and pondered the things Sara said. Until tonight he hadn't realized the resentment and doubt she carried with her all these years. She thought he didn't want to be around her. How wrong she was. If he'd known about her, nothing could have kept him away from her.

He heard his daughter's voice drifting from the other room, and picked up a distinct word here and there, but not enough to make any sense out of the conversation.

Five minutes later, she called out, "I'm off now, Sam. Let's start the movie."

He stepped into the living room and eased himself down on the couch. "How's your mother?"

She looked at him and wiped a hand across her moist eyes. "She misses me and wishes I wasn't stuck here with you."

The words cut deep and grazed Sam's defenses. He wanted to tell her Linda is who decided to leave and move hundreds of miles away, but he refrained. Why add more pain for his little girl to deal with? He looked at his silent daughter's sad face. The resentment inside him grew claws and threatened to squeeze off his air.

Whatever Linda said to Sara changed her whole demeanor. She no longer wanted to talk to him. She pulled back inside her shell like a frightened turtle. What would cause a mother to deliberately say things she knew would hurt her own child? Sam sighed and tapped the start button on the remote.

CHAPTER TEN

Abby stretched in her chair and rubbed her eyes. She had a full blown headache and the words on the computer screen blurred. The later the afternoon grew, the less able she was to keep her mind focused. She opened her desk drawer and pulled out a bottle of aspirin.

Thoughts of Sam swirled through her aching head. He had joined her in the cafeteria at lunch and asked her out for the third time in the past three weeks. For the third time she declined. Not that she didn't want to go out with him, she did. She liked Sam. Enough that she could fall in love with him if she let herself. She couldn't risk it. She knew what could happen if you push back your dreams and goals. Yes, it would be safer to keep her distance, but also lonelier.

Abby's head pulsed, pulling her back to the moment. She rested her elbows on the desk, placed her fingertips on her temples and made slow circular motions.

"Headache?"

Abby turned. Clark stood in the doorway. "Yeah. I've been fighting it all afternoon," she said.

Clark smiled and walked up to her and set a bouquet of golden asters on her desk, then slid into a chair. "Pretty flowers for a pretty lady." He winked.

The professor was persistent; she had to give him that. "They're beautiful. Thank you, just what I need today."

"What you need is a good stiff shot of caffeine to get rid of that headache."

"Yeah, it might help. But I don't have time for a break. I've got a ton of paperwork to muddle through before I leave this afternoon."

Clark pushed back in his chair and stood. "Sit tight. I'll fetch you a cup, with lots of cream." He smiled and strode toward the door.

"Thanks." Abby watched him go and wondered why she couldn't feel the attraction for him she felt for Sam. He was a nice person, considerate too. But he wasn't Sam. She sighed and tried to ignore her pounding head as she swiveled her chair back to the computer.

* * *

Two hours later, Abby walked into her kitchen and pulled a frozen dinner from the freezer. She was in no mood to cook for herself.

She checked her voice mail. No messages. Emily hadn't tried to call. Though Abby was angry with her sister, she missed her. Emily was always a constant in her life. Her sister was always there for her.

She picked up the phone to call her sister, then laid it down when she flashed on the scene they had at their moms. She was in such a funk and didn't want to say something that might make matters worse. Tomorrow she would make the call, she half-heartedly promised herself.

The microwave pinged and she jumped. She took the dinner from the oven and sat down to watch TV. The local evening news did nothing to lighten her mood and when she finished the mediocre meal she busied herself with the endless list of to-do preparations for the big sendoff she was putting together for Carrie's going-away-to-college party at the end of August. The biggest project was planning the menu for one hundred fifty guests.

She worked nonstop for nearly three hours, but by ten o'clock she was snuggled in bed with a Robin Cook classic in her hand. The lamp on the nightstand gave a soft glow to the pages of the well-worn book. She'd read *Coma* more times than she could recall, but never tired of the author's uncanny way he made his thrillers come to life.

Over an hour later, the doorbell rang, interrupting her at the precise time Susan Wheeler, a third year medical student, climbed through the ceiling tiles at Boston Memorial Hospital.

She dog-eared the book, laid it down and slipped from the bed, and wondered who would ring her bell at this hour. She rarely had visitors, and certainly not this late. She pulled on a robe and padded barefoot to the door. One hand on the knob, she leaned in and put her right eye to the peephole, then took a step back. Emily. Oh great.

She opened the door and looked from her sister's face to the duffle bag she clutched tightly in her hand. "You're out late."

"Did I wake you?" Emily asked.

Abby shook her head. "No. I was reading." Abby shifted from one foot to the other. "I was gonna call you."

"Sure you were."

Well, I was, Abby thought and bit back an irritated retort.

"Are you going to ask me to come in or what?"

"Sure." Abby blinked. "Come in."

Emily stepped across the threshold and set her carryall just inside the door.

Abby's eyes narrowed. "What's with the bag?"

"I need a place to crash." Emily walked into the living room and plopped on the couch.

"Why?" Abby sat in the chair across from her sister.

"I've got to sort things out, figure out what I'm going to do."

"What things?"

"Trust me, it's complicated," Emily said.

Trust her? Right. Abby scrutinized her sister. She was a mess. Her hair looked like a comb hadn't seen it all day. She had on an oversized T-shirt that she more than likely weaseled from Dad. Emily was always into helping herself to other people's clothes.

"Can I stay with you for a while… just until I can figure out what I'm going to do?" Emily asked.

"Here?" Abby stared at her sister.

Emily shrugged. "I don't have anywhere else to go."

"Does Mom know you're here?"

"I didn't tell her." Emily shifted positions and Abby noticed her visitor's hands were a little shaky. "But she knows I always come to you when I'm in trouble."

Abby gathered in a long breath. What had her sister done this time? "Okay, Emily, out with it. What's going on?"

Emily caught her lower lip between her teeth. She sat there, silent, and blinked several times.

"Come on. Talk to me."

"Well." Her sister hesitated and tugged at the hem of her shirt. "I think… No, I'm sure about it because I missed… I got a test at Walmart and, well it was positive. I'm pregnant."

What? It took a moment to process Emily's words. Then, in a sudden flash, a vibration of understanding swept over her, and made the hairs stand up on her arms as her mind registered the information. Her breath jammed in her throat, she struggled to swallow.

"It's Robert's baby," Abby said, barely above a whisper.

Emily nodded. "I'm sorry…"

"You're sorry?"

"I am, believe me."

"You swore to me that you and Robert were just friends." Abby huffed out an irritated breath. "Quite a friendship you two have going on."

Emily closed her eyes and in that action Abby

saw herself. They were alike in so many ways. They both wanted to shut out the world when they didn't like what they saw.

"Why didn't you just tell me the truth?" Frustration nipped at Abby's words. "I had the right to know."

Emily's fingers sank into the plush arm of the sofa. She opened her eyes and looked at Abby. "I was afraid you'd think I let you down."

Resentment rippled through Abby. She glared at her sister. "Ya think?"

"I never meant to hurt you." Emily's breath hitched. "Never."

"You never mean to do anything, do you? You act first and think later."

Abby stood, strode to the window and stared out at the lamppost on the corner. She'd moved to Tampa to get away from her past, from reminders of her life with Robert. She turned and looked at her sister. "I don't need this. I'm trying to make a new life for myself. Now you show up and dump this bomb in my lap." Abby pulled her hair back from her face and held it. "And you actually have the nerve to ask me if you can stay here?"

"Please, Abby." Emily looked down at her feet. "You're all I've got now. Mom is furious. She practically kicked me out."

Abby shook her head. "Mom wouldn't do that."

"Not to you or Carrie. She's different with me."

"Whatever," Abby said. She didn't want to go down that worn path. "What about Robert? Where does he fit in?"

"We're fighting. He says I got pregnant on

purpose to force him to marry me."

"Well, did you?"

Emily shook her head. "No. Of course not." Tears welled in her eyes. "I wouldn't sink that low." She dug a tissue from her purse, blew her nose. "I thought he loved me."

Been there, done that, Abby thought.

"Come on sis, have a heart. Just let me stay here for a little while," Emily said. "I'll make other arrangements as soon as I can."

With a sense of foreboding Abby sank into the chair she'd vacated. Why did this happen to her? Why couldn't Emily take her problems and go somewhere else, preferably far away, to solve them? Emily should be in her own home, taking care of her own dilemma. Instead, here she was, in the middle of her safe haven. Good grief, I moved to Tampa to get away from anything and everything that involved Robert, she thought.

She glanced at Emmy huddled on the couch, looking like the little girl who always ran to her older sister to fix everything. Only this time she couldn't fix it.

Abby sighed. "Okay, you can stay. Just until you can make other arrangements. But I want you to know one thing; I will not allow Robert back in my life." Even as the words slid off her tongue, her internal alarm kicked on and blasted shrieks of warning through her brain.

Emily sighed and leaned back on the couch. "Thank you, Abby. You won't regret this."

She already regretted it.

Abby stood and motioned for Emily to follow as

she walked to the spare bedroom. "There's fresh linen on the bed, and extra covers in the hall closet."

Emily tried to smile, but Abby caught the glint of moisture in her eyes. "Try to get some rest. Things will look better in the morning."

"Thanks for letting me stay."

Abby nodded, then turned and walked back to her bedroom. She stepped inside and shut the door. She strode to her bedside and picked up her book and tossed it on the nightstand. So much for reading. She'd never be able to concentrate now. She flipped on the TV and plopped on the bed. Why couldn't she get away from her past?

She buried her head in her hands and let the realization fully sink in; Emily pregnant and Robert the father. Robert would now be an intruding part of the Dennison family forever, no matter how hard she tried to distance herself. Pain clutched her heart and unseen fingers squeezed until she could feel a physical ache. Her eyes filled with tears that spilled over and ran down her cheeks.

She picked up her pillow, held it close, rocked it back and forth like she used to rock Emily when she ran into Abby's bedroom in the middle of the night, in tears from a bad dream. Emily trusted her sister and felt she had the power to make the boogie man go away. She must still believe it.

Her headache returned full force. She blamed Emily for everything.

* * *

Early Friday morning, Sam set the spray bottle

of window cleaner on his utility cart and pushed a strand of hair off his forehead with the back of his wrist. He stepped back and studied his work. The glass in the front door of the atrium glistened.

Abby walked up the steps and he grinned as he eased open the door and held it while she stepped across the threshold. "Hey, Abby."

"Good morning." Her face didn't reflect anything good about the morning. Her expressive eyes were dark and troubled and the dusky circles under them worried him.

"You okay?"

Abby pursed her lips and nodded. "I'm fine. Running a little late." She glanced at her watch. "Actually a lot late. Gotta go." She turned and walked away.

His gaze followed her down the corridor that bustled with staff and students. He rubbed his jaw, confused. Abby was never late. He wheeled his cart to the windows adjacent to the door, picked up the spray bottle and aimed the nozzle. He pondered his attraction for Abby as he made wide circular motions on the glass with his rag. Though he'd never verbalized his feelings, he liked her, liked her a lot. He didn't think he was in love with her yet but he was rapidly falling. As for Abby, more and more he was convinced she felt the same way, but something held her back. Even after she'd refused his date invitations, he didn't doubt the magnetism between them. He was not going to give up on her without a fight.

Thoughts of Abby stayed with him all day and at quitting time he found himself at the deli. He ordered sandwiches and chips for two.

Food in tow, Sam walked to Abby's office and knocked on the door, determined.

"Come in," she called.

Sam sucked in a long breath, opened the door and stepped inside. "I've got sandwiches and chips." He held up his brown bag special. "You seemed so down this morning. I'm here to cheer you up."

"Oh, Sam, that's so sweet."

He felt heat rush up his neck as her words warmed him, but he hid their effect with a grin.

Abby looked at her watch. "But I really should go home."

"You've got to eat, don't you? Might as well do it with me." He walked to her side and motioned for her to stand.

Abby stood and placed her hands on her hips and cocked her head to the side.

Sam winked. "Don't worry, I'm not kidnapping you."

Abby gave him a piercing gaze, but her lips turned up at the corners.

"We're going to the lake and have a nice picnic," Sam said, trying to make his voice sound authoritative. "And I'm not taking no for an answer."

"Really I–"

He held up a hand to halt her protest. "Come on, it'll do you good." He nudged her toward the door. "No arguments. I'm the doctor."

"I guess you are." She chuckled and he couldn't help staring down at her, at the warmth in her eyes as her gaze met his. They shared a long look, then headed down the hall.

A few minutes later, they sat on a bench facing the lake and Sam doled out the food. The soft breeze from the north cooled the hint of perspiration on his neck and face. He caught a spicy floral scent in the air. They shared easy banter as they ate their chips and roast beef subs.

Sam swallowed the last bite of his sandwich and cleared his throat. "What's bothering you, Abby?" He straightened his shoulders and leveled a look at her. "Is it me? Have I done something to offend you?"

Abby shook her head. "No, Sam. It's not you." She sighed. "It's Emily."

Sam raised a brow. "Something else happen?"

"Oh yeah." She rolled her eyes.

Sam laced his fingers together, leaned back and gave Abby a few moments to collect her thoughts. The lake, only a few feet in front of them, glistened beyond the thick, green lawn. Snow-white swans floated across its smooth surface. Abby seemed to be studying the landscape, but her eyes finally got to him. "Do you want to talk about it?" he asked.

She drew in a long breath and blew it out, making her hair lift off her forehead. "Emily is camped out at my condo."

"Is that right?" he said, feeling as though he'd missed something important. Last time he'd heard, the sisters weren't speaking.

"Believe me." Abby flicked a couple crumbs off her thigh. "It wasn't my idea."

"How long will she stay?"

Abby shrugged. "Who knows? With my sister anything's possible."

"Well, that'll give you guys a chance to…"

"She's pregnant," Abby blurted out, "and Robert's the father. You know, my ex-boyfriend, the guy Emily swore was just a *friend.*"

Sam inhaled sharply. He wondered what that would mean for Abby. How would she cope? "I'm sorry. That has to bite."

Abby shrugged. "As mad as I am at Emily, I still don't want him hurting her." Abby huffed out a breath, obviously upset. "And he will, you know. He's a user."

Sam looked at her hands. They were balled into fists. His eyes moved to her face. "He really hurt you, huh?"

Abby nodded. She tucked her hair behind her ear and gazed out at the lake.

"How long were you with him?"

"Seven years."

Sam whistled. "That's a long time."

"Too long." Abby was silent a moment and her eyes filled with tears. When she spoke, it was in the low tones of recounted memory. "Four of those years we lived together." She paused, glanced at Sam as if she expected him to think less of her. He didn't.

She continued. "I felt guilty the entire time. God was dealing with me, showing me I was in a relationship I shouldn't be in. I should have listened to Him but I was so wrapped up in Robert. You know the old cliché; I thought I couldn't live without him."

"Sometimes it's hard to walk away," he said.

Abby turned to him and she looked so vulnerable. He saw pain flicker across her face. "It was for me," she said. "I was naïve enough to think he'd marry me. I kept hanging on, waiting for him to commit. Of course, that never happened. When I finally told Robert I couldn't live with him anymore until we were married, I honestly thought he'd be okay with it. You know, show me a little understanding. But he didn't. He moved out that night."

Moisture clung to Abby's eyelids. Sam's heart ached for her but he was pleased that she trusted him enough to open up about her past. He pulled a napkin from the lunch bag and handed it to her. She dabbed her eyes.

"I let Robert manipulate me into doing things that went against everything I believed in. I compromised all my beliefs for one man."

He noticed her eyes grew distant, and he saw a flash of regret echoed in their depths.

"I compromised my faith, my dignity," Abby said. "I really loved him that much."

Sam closed his eyes at the sadness in her words. No wonder she wasn't anxious to get involved with another man. He wanted to hold her to him, tell her he realized how difficult it had been for her, and that she'd triumphed over the biggest adversary of all...herself. Though it was painful, she'd surrendered to God.

"I know it's hard for you to talk about this," he said.

Abby nodded. "Talking about it brings back all

the dirty feelings I had about myself after he walked out. The reason I left Orlando was to get away from all the reminders of that bad time. I just wanted to forget about it."

"Now Emily's in love with him."

"Oh, yeah. That's what hurts so much. She saw what I went through after Robert left me, how devastated I was. I would think she'd never put herself in a position of getting involved with her own sister's nemesis."

"And you can't forgive her?"

"I want to. I really do. I don't want to feel the anger, but I don't know how to let it go."

"Sometimes forgiveness is hard. But it's what God calls us to do. Harboring a grudge doesn't hurt the other person. It hurts you a lot more than it hurts them."

"Sam." Abby met his gaze and the gentleness of her expression expanded into her voice. "Are you speaking from experience?"

He nodded. "Yes, Linda. I couldn't forgive her for keeping Sara from me. My anger escalated to the point I actually hated her, wanted to get back at her, to make her suffer like she'd made me suffer. Then when I became a Christian, a good friend counseled me, and made me realize I only hurt myself with all my negative feelings."

"So you're over it now? No more hate for the woman that lied to you in the worst way?"

"I've forgiven her and don't harbor any revenge. Abby, what she did was wrong. Forgiveness doesn't mean that you think the person's actions were okay or that you condone their behavior. It just means you can let it go, get on with your life."

"I'm glad you were able to find the strength to work through it."

"Forgiveness is a choice, but it takes God to give you the strength to let go of the anger so He can heal you."

Abby closed her eyes and rested her head against the hard bench. "My mind knows that, but my heart can't grasp it yet."

"It will. Give it some time." He raked his fingers through his hair. "I wish there was something I could do to help you."

"You already have." A smile tipped up the corners of her lips. "It's easy to talk to you. Thank you. I'm glad you insisted on the picnic. It gave me a pleasant interlude in the midst of all this craziness."

"My pleasure." Sam gave her a grin. He stood. "Come on, let's go for a walk."

CHAPTER ELEVEN

Abby slipped from the bench and fell in step with Sam. They walked along the shore by the lake as the gentle wind whispered through her hair. The sand tickled her toes in her thrifty bargain-table Coach sandals.

A light, cool breeze replaced the oppressive heat of earlier as thunder rumbled faintly in the distance. She gathered in a long, deep breath and the distinct smell of the coming rain wafted over her.

Sam seemed to feel it too. "We're in for some showers tonight." The corners of his mouth turned up exposing straight white teeth.

Abby nodded and pushed her hair behind her ear. As she walked close to his side, she responded to his grin, his deep blue eyes that crinkled at the edges when a smile lit up his face. She got a rush. Warmth crawled up her neck like the cozy feeling of peace that followed a shared kiss with someone special. The air was electric and not only with the storm.

Sam stopped and turned toward her. His eyes narrowed a fraction as he looked at her. The flicker of some emotion, she couldn't define, produced a subtle shift in his expression. He reached for her hand then laced his fingers with hers and gave a little squeeze.

She looked down at their intertwined fingers. She thought of her Savior's nail-scarred hands. It was strange, almost eerie for a second. Like the hands were keys to a hidden meaning that swirled around in her head just out of reach. She felt a chill and pulled free.

"Are you all right?" The warmth and caring in Sam's eyes touched a raw, aching place in her soul.

"Sure," Abby said, and looked away. She felt off-balance and in desperate need of something solid and safe and dependable to cling to, something or someone.

Someone like Sam.

Even as the thought darted across her mind, she dismissed it as absurd. The man was wrong for her, yet she couldn't dismiss as easily the chemistry between them.

If only he wanted more children.

She needed to stop the mixed signals she sent him. It wasn't fair to him, or to her. She wanted to run away from her past *and* her future. What was wrong with her?

An awkward moment hung between them as they continued to walk. Then Sam spoke. "I'm sorry if I was out of line." His voice was husky and she guessed he was feeling what she was feeling. "I didn't mean to offend you."

Abby shook her head and looked up at him. "You didn't."

They stopped at the end of the path and turned to retrace their steps. A couple in the middle of the lake caught Abby's attention as they paddled their canoe toward the far shore. They turned and waved. Sam and Abby returned the gesture.

"That's Fred, our trainer, and his wife, Sharon," Sam said. "Looks like they're calling it a day."

"How'd they get out there? I never noticed them before."

"They put their canoe in at the dock on the other side. The only way to access the lake from this side is on foot, or with my golf cart. That's why I like to come here. It's private."

"Do the kids hang out on the other side?"

Sam shook his head. "No, the kids don't hang out at the lake. They prefer the gulf." Sam chuckled. "That's fine by me."

"Yeah. But they sure don't know what they're missing."

Abby bent down, removed her sandal and shook out sand, then slipped her foot back inside. "How are things going with Sara?"

A shrug lifted Sam's shoulders. "Sometimes I think we make progress, then other times I just don't know. She can really throw out an attitude."

"Don't give up on her." Abby's stomach tightened at the memory of Sara's cold eyes and red, defiant face when she almost dared Abby to tell Sam about the birth control pills.

"I think she might be smoking, or hanging around with people who do."

"Oh yeah?" Abby cringed as she flashed on Brenda's pack of cigarettes. She toyed with the idea of telling Sam. No, that would still be a violation of confidentiality even if by a long stretch.

"I've caught a whiff of smoke on her. More than once."

"Have you asked her about it?"

"No. It's so faint I'm not really sure." He scratched his head. "Maybe I'm just imagining it. And if I'm wrong and ask her about it she'll go off on me. I don't want to chance losing more ground with her."

Abby stopped and regarded him. "You're a good father. Anyone can see that. Just do what comes naturally and be as honest as you can without belittling her feelings."

He shook his head. "I wish I could get this parent thing down right."

"I think you do a great job."

"Thanks." He blew out a breath. "I hope we have a good weekend," he said, but his voice didn't offer much hope.

Abby saw a flash of lightning in the distance, and a few seconds later thunder crackled before it settled into a loud rumble that threatened a storm. The sky grew dark with gray billowing clouds that completely obliterated the sun, already sinking fast in the west. "I think we need to head back before we get drenched."

Sam nodded. "Yeah, looks like it's moving in fast."

Just then the first raindrop hit Abby in the forehead with a splat. She looked at Sam and they both burst out in laughter as they sprinted to the golf cart.

* * *

Saturday morning Abby woke to the sounds of a sick sister. She sat up in bed, stretched and yawned as her brain processed what her ears picked up. Poor Emmy. She popped from the bed and slipped her arms through the sleeves of a pink cotton robe, then walked to the bathroom and tapped on the door. "You okay?"

"Uh huh." Emily opened the door a few inches, stuck her head out, a wet washrag pressed to her forehead. "Morning sickness is not fun."

"I don't imagine. Do you want a cup of tea and some toast?"

"Yeah, I'll take some toast." She shook her head. "But no tea. Do you have bottled water?"

Abby nodded and eyed her sister. Her hair was plastered to her head and without makeup her eyes were lackluster, dark circles underneath. She must be exhausted.

"Sure you don't want to try some tea?" Abby asked.

"No. I don't want any tea. Give it a rest. Pregnant women know what they do or do not want."

"Sorry." Abby shrugged. "But I've never been pregnant before."

Emily waved her off with a dismissive hand. "I'm going to take a quick shower. See you in ten." She pulled the door shut.

Abby padded into the kitchen and flipped on the coffee maker. She pulled the loaf of wheat bread from the cabinet and took out two slices, slipped them in the toaster.

A few minutes later Emily stepped into the room, and plopped down at the table. She crossed her legs and pushed damp hair off her forehead. Her eyes were brighter and some color had returned to her cheeks.

"Sorry I was so grumpy before," Emily said.

"No problem." Abby pushed down the lever on the toaster. "How's your stomach?"

"Better. The first thing in the morning is the worst. By noon I'm starved, feeling like I could eat a horse."

Abby chuckled. "Try putting some saltines on your nightstand when you go to bed. The next morning you can nibble on some crackers before you get up. That's supposed to help. Or so I've heard."

"Sure. I'll try anything."

The toaster gave up its bounty. Abby spread a tad of butter on the toast, set it on a plate and handed it to Emily along with cold bottled water.

"Thanks." Emily twisted off the lid, and took a sip. She broke off small pieces of her almost dry toast and cautiously slipped bites into her mouth, chewing each piece slowly and deliberately.

Abby filled a mug with steaming coffee, dumped in half-and-half until the coffee turned golden, stirred and tapped the spoon against the side of the mug, then placed the spoon in the stainless steel sink. Wrapping her fingers around the mug handle, she walked to the table and set the cup down.

"The toast helping?" Abby asked.

"Yeah. I think I'm fine now."

"I'm having a bowl of corn flakes." Abby turned and opened the pantry. "Want some?"

"Better not. Maybe later."

Abby grabbed the milk from the refrigerator and poured a white stream over her cereal. "I have my riding lesson at ten, but I'll be home by noon. Do you want to hit the mall with me this afternoon?"

"Okay. I need to look at maternity clothes. My pants are getting pretty snug." Emily took a sip from her water and looked at Abby over the bottle. "You and Sam are getting pretty tight, aren't you?"

"Sam's a good friend." Abby carried her bowl to the table.

Emily raised her eyebrows and shot her a look. "Good friend? I thought you really went for him."

Abby shrugged.

"What?"

"It's complicated."

"I don't see what the problem is…" Emily's phone rang and she pulled it from her pocket, looked at the ID. Her face turned pink and she sprang up from her chair. "I'll be right back," she said and stepped from the room.

Abby shoved the last bite of cereal into her mouth and pushed back from the table. She walked to the sink, rinsed the bowl and popped it in the dishwasher, then headed toward her bedroom.

In the hallway, Emily's voice drifted from her room, clear and distinct. She sounded like she was crying. Abby paused and heard, "I can't do that,

Robert. I won't." It made Abby nauseous and she wasn't pregnant. Emily's words continued, "You know I'd do anything for you, but not that."

Renewed anger hit Abby hard. It threatened to bury her like an avalanche. She didn't want to hear anymore. She gritted her teeth and sped to her room. She stepped into shorts and pulled a T-shirt over her head then slipped into flip-flops and headed out the back door.

She kicked off her shoes where the grass ended and the sand began and walked barefoot on the beach, letting the waves caress her feet. Why, of all people, did Emily pick Robert to be involved with? If the situation were reversed, she would never get involved with someone that had hurt Emily. Never. It goes to show you where Emily's loyalties lie, certainly not with me, Abby thought.

She picked up speed as she plodded through the moist sand, going farther and farther down the beach until she reached the parking lot at the complex's fitness center. Her anger smoldered as she stepped onto the cement, warm and inviting against the soles of her feet. What she needed was a good workout on the treadmill, to run until she was too breathless to think. She sure couldn't do it barefoot.

Resentment funneled through her. She hated feeling like this. Overall she felt a lot worse than she did when she lived in Orlando. What good did it do to move here, she thought, if she couldn't shake her past?

Out of nowhere, Sam's words about forgiveness played through her mind. She stopped, plopped down on the curb and dropped her head into her hands. "Oh, God, please help me. Please take this anger from my heart. I love my sister but I'm so mad at her I can't think straight."

* * *

Abby handled Hero like a pro. She didn't need any more lessons from Sam. But he didn't want to admit that. The lessons were the only alone time he had with her.

"How's it going with Emily?" he asked as they dismounted and led the horses through the paddock gate.

"Robert called her this morning and I guess they argued. She was upset and cried."

Sam looked at her. "How are you holding up?"

Abby shrugged. "I'm hanging in." She glanced at him, a soft laugh whispered at her lips. "I took your advice and prayed about it."

"Good for you."

"What can I say? You're a good influence on me, doctor."

Sam gave her a wink. "You can't go wrong with me."

"You think?" Abby chuckled and gave his shoulder a little push.

Sam liked the feel of Abby's hand on his shoulder, even if it was all in fun. The way he felt must have been reflected in his eyes because Abby's cheeks grew pink and she turned away then cleared her throat.

"What about Sara?" Abby asked a few beats

later. "Are things getting any better?"

Sam pulled the saddle from Savannah and laid it on a bench. "She's spending the weekend with me and I didn't have to tie her up to get her to agree."

"Well, that's a start." Abby rubbed Hero's muzzle and he gave her hand a gentle nudge.

"I don't know. She barely spoke to me last night."

"She's been through a lot in the last few weeks." Abby shook her head. "I can only imagine how I'd feel if my mother moved away when I was fourteen."

Sam nodded. "She won't admit it, but I know it devastated her when Linda left. And she doesn't trust me. She's put a barrier between us, and to save me, I can't get through it."

"That's too bad. I wish she could see you through my eyes."

Abby's gentle words tugged at his heart, and a warm tingle rushed through his veins. He turned toward her and gave her a slow smile. "What would I do without you?"

"Oh, you'd manage just fine." She chuckled but Sam heard the slight unsteadiness in her voice. Her gaze met his and he was sure he could see longing in her eyes. He wanted to take her in his arms and hug her to him, tell her no, he would not manage fine without her. But he didn't.

The horses, unfettered, moseyed across the corral. Sam stepped through the gate and followed Abby across the grass to the parking lot. He opened her car door and held it while she slipped into the seat. "Same time next Saturday?"

She hesitated, then nodded as she pulled the door shut.

Sam slid behind the steering wheel of his car and watched Abby turn left out of the parking lot. He fired up the engine and headed home, his head spinning with thoughts of a perky little nurse who inched her way into his heart more and more with each day.

A few minutes later Sam stepped through his front door. Sara was up. He could tell by the appearance of his living room, her paraphernalia strewn everywhere. Why was his child so messy?

"Did you have a good time with your girlfriend?" she asked, as she looked up from the couch where she cradled her phone near her ear.

He sighed and walked over to her. "We had a nice ride."

"Eww." She wrinkled up her nose. "You smell like a horse."

"Yeah." He chuckled and ruffled her hair. "Great aroma, huh?"

Sara pulled her head back. "Disgusting."

"I'll grab a quick shower, then I'll hustle up something for lunch."

"Don't hurry. I scrambled some eggs earlier."

Sam winced. He did not look forward to the mess she no doubt left in the other room. He'd deal with that after he cleaned up.

Twenty minutes later, Sam, freshly showered and shaved, headed to the kitchen. He stopped in the doorway and looked at his daughter. "Sure you're not hungry?"

Sara shook her head. "You don't have to wait on

me. I can take care of myself."

Yeah, right, Sam thought as he stepped into the messy kitchen. He loaded the dishwasher, wiped off the stove and countertops then threw together a ham and cheese sandwich before he joined his daughter. "What are you watching?"

Sara shrugged. "Some dumb movie. Nothing else on."

"You want to go somewhere, do something?"

Sara glared at him. "Like what, Sam?"

"Oh, I don't know. How about skating?"

She rolled her eyes. "Oh yeah, that sounds like a blast."

"Well, you come up with an idea then. I'm open to suggestions."

Sara huffed out an annoyed breath and shot up from the couch. "I've got some homework I need to do." She walked down the hall, her head buried in her phone.

Sam sighed. He flipped the channel to ESPN. He might as well catch up on some sports scores since his daughter didn't seem to want to spend time with him. He couldn't focus. His mind wandered for nearly an hour before he gave it up and hit the off button on the remote.

He stood and nearly tripped over Sara's backpack by the end table. Some papers fell out. He stooped and gathered them up, pulled open the zipper and slid them inside. His gaze fell on a pack of birth control pills. He did a double take.

He pulled in a long breath. Surely, they didn't belong to his daughter. He looked at the pack and read: *Sara Tennyson: Take one daily.* His gut clenched into a knot, and an unsettling feeling of apprehension swept over him. *No, God, please. Not my little girl.*

He walked into Sara's bedroom. She was propped on the bed, knees drawn up, still engrossed with her cell.

"What's this?" Sam extended his hand.

Sara looked up. He saw surprise ripple across her face, followed by a scowl. "What were you doing snooping in my stuff?"

"I wasn't snooping for your information. I was picking up after you." He stepped toward her. "Well?"

Sara shrugged. "It's no big deal."

"Stop it, Sara. Right now. This is definitely a big deal." He waved the pack of Tricyclen in the air. "Where did you get these?"

"Maybe Mom isn't the only one keeping secrets." She shot him a glare. "If you want to know where I got them why don't you ask your precious little nurse?"

Sam dropped his arm to his side and took a step back. He couldn't believe Abby would do this behind his back. He shook his head. "No. Abby wouldn't have…"

"I guess all the women in your life are full of surprises."

He pinned Sara with an intent look. "I don't know how to get through to you. God knows, I've tried. But I keep…"

"You should have thought about that before you made me stay here and not go with my mother."

"What's that supposed to mean?"

Sara huffed. "Mom told me all about it. How you threatened to take her to court if she didn't let me stay here. And you, being the all-important doctor, scared her off."

Sam shook his head. "You've got it all wrong. But we'll get into that later." He pointed to the door. "Get to the car."

"Why... Where are we going?"

"Abby's."

CHAPTER TWELVE

After the riding lesson with Sam, Abby fished keys from her purse and with a shaky hand turned the ignition and put the gear in drive. She could feel his eyes as they penetrated the back of her head while she drove across the parking lot. She sensed Sam was willing and ready to step up their relationship to the next level. She could not go there, but Lord knew she wanted to.

Her fingers gripped the steering wheel. As painful as it was for her, she had to pull away from him because she was unwilling to embrace the sacrifice that she'd have to make if she committed to him. She could not, would not, give up her hopes for a child.

Abby turned right on Taney Boulevard and headed to her apartment. The noon-time traffic was heavy and the drive was a little slow. Her mind shifted gears to the problems that awaited her at her condo. For the first time since she moved to Tampa, she dreaded going home. She was already in need of a reprieve from Emily and what her presence represented.

She hated being thrown in the middle of Emily's and Robert's problems. She pursed her lips and glanced in the rearview mirror. Her own tormented eyes stared back at her.

And all at once an insight jolted her.

The safe, predictable world she'd created for herself by moving away from Orlando hadn't simply vanished in a heartbeat, leaving her exposed and vulnerable. She was fooling herself to believe relocating could erase the past or heal her heart. You can't run from the past, some distant voice in her brain announced, and try as she might she couldn't chase the truth away. She sniffed and turned the car into her drive, cut the engine and walked to the door.

A bubbly Emily was waiting for her in the living room. She tossed her People magazine on the end table and popped up from the couch. "Still up for shopping?" she asked.

Emily was dressed in form-fitting jeans and a pastel blue top. Her hair, pulled back in a ponytail, complimented her high cheek bones. To look at her you'd never guess she was twenty-eight. She looked more like eighteen.

"You know me, I'm always ready for the mall." Abby chuckled. "But what about lunch? I'm starved."

"I'm craving tacos. And we can get them at the mall."

"That's why you're in such a hurry to get going." Abby laughed. "It's not my titillating company. I'm hurt."

"You've found me out." Emily laughed aloud. "I can't slip anything by you."

"Well, come on, let's get going." Abby opened the front door and the two sisters walked side by side to her Taurus.

On the ride to the mall, Emily plied her with questions about Sam and she was able to conjure up a few stories about the riding lessons that elicited some laughter. Abby was careful to avoid any details that might expose her frayed emotions. She wasn't ready to share her dilemma with the sister who turned traitor in a heartbeat.

The first thing they did after they found a parking spot and walked what seemed like a block to the entrance, was get in line at Taco Hut. Emily ordered a Double Decker Taco Supreme and Abby opted for a Cheesy Bean and Rice Burrito.

They found an empty table and opened their food. "I'm as hungry as you." Abby chuckled. "And I can't blame it on pregnancy."

"You're always hungry." Emily shook her head. "It amazes me how you can stay so slim and eat the way you do."

Abby shrugged. "What can I say? It's a curse."

"Yeah, right. Wish I had a curse like that."

Abby took a bite of rice and beans. When she looked up she spotted Clark in the line. An attractive, petite brunette, dressed in a yellow-flowered sundress and open-toed white sandals with at least three inch heels, clung to his right arm. When they retrieved their order they turned and headed to a table and slid into chairs directly in front of Abby.

Clark set the food down and glanced toward her. She saw surprise flick across his face. He cleared his throat.

"Hello, Abby," Clark said. He gave her a half grin. "Nice to see you."

Abby nodded and swallowed down her bite. "Hi Clark."

He glanced toward Emily, and Abby made the introductions.

"Hey," Emily said.

Clark paused, his smile fading. "Good to meet you, Emily." He motioned to the brunette. "This is Sherri Brownfield…"

"Nice to meet you guys," Sherri said. She looked at Clark and gave him a long, slow smile. "Clark's going to let me pick out something from Macy's today."

"How nice," Abby said and was a little ashamed when she heard how shallow her words sounded. She thought about asking Sherri if he brought her a bouquet of flowers and coffee with lots of cream. She stifled the impulse. It wasn't worth the effort. Besides, she was not jealous, she told herself.

A red glow spread across Clark's face. "Today's her birthday."

"Mmm." Abby gave him her best smile as the two turned and focused on their food.

"He's kinda cute," Emily said as she popped a bite of taco into her mouth.

Abby shrugged. "I guess."

"What's the problem?" Emily looked at the couple at the other table, then back to Abby.

"Men." Abby shook her head. "He's been coming on to me ever since I started at Brighton."

"You're kidding!"

"Am not." Abby rolled her eyes. "He even brought me a bouquet Monday."

"That's hilarious." Emily laid down the taco and stared at her. "You weren't falling for him were you?"

Abby swallowed a gulp of her tea. "No. But you know what's pathetic? I was feeling bad because I wasn't interested in him." She laughed. "I'm so gullible."

"You're not either." Emily wiped her mouth on her napkin. "Let's finish up and get out of here."

"Good idea." She took a bite of her burrito, gave Clark a once-over and chided herself because she thought he had a thing for her. She decided it was providence she ran in to him today. Now she didn't have to worry about the lonely professor's feelings. She tamped down a chuckle. He'd be just fine without her.

* * *

Abby and Emily toted armfuls of shopping bags into Abby's condo and set them in the foyer. Abby blew out a breath and motioned toward the packages. "I didn't need all this stuff."

"Yeah," Emily said. "We really went overboard."

"Ya think?" Abby laughed. They walked into the kitchen and Abby pulled the coffee from the cabinet. "I'll make hot chocolate for you."

159

"Great."

Abby held the pot under the faucet and turned on the tap. The doorbell chimed. "Get that, will you?"

"I'm on it," Emily said over her shoulder as she headed to the front door.

Abby spooned three large tablespoons of coffee into the filter, slid it into the coffeemaker and poured in a carafe of water. After she flipped on the machine, she wiped her hands on a dishtowel and headed to the foyer to see who dropped by.

She stopped short when she heard Robert's voice, low and husky. "Abortion is the only thing that's going to fix this for us, Emily. You know we can't…"

Abby stepped around the corner, incensed. She gathered all the strength she could muster to not tell him to get out of her house. "You've got to be kidding."

He turned and gave her a big grin. "Hi, Abs."

Abs? She ignored his greeting.

"I'm trying to talk some sense into your bullheaded sister," Robert said, and nodded toward Emily.

"I'm not bullheaded." Emily shot Robert a look that seared. Then she glanced at Abby. "I guess you heard. He wants me to get an abortion."

Abby fumed. "Yeah, I heard." She glared at her ex. "How could you even suggest such a thing?"

"Neither one of us wants a baby right now, not that it's any of your business," Robert said, his tone kicked up an octave. "If she was more responsible, this wouldn't have happened."

"It takes two, you know," Abby told him through

clenched teeth. "If you…"

Emily laid a hand on Abby's arm and glared at Robert. "Oh, yeah. Blame me. It's all my fault. You had nothing in it right?"

Robert's ears turned pink. "Just get rid of it."

"Not an 'it'." Emily sighed. "A baby."

"Your baby," Abby reminded him. "A living, breathing, tiny human being."

"You can't call it a baby. It's not reached viability."

Abby shook her head. "Life begins at conception."

"You might be the nurse." Robert's words snapped like a steel trap. "But I'm not completely ignorant."

That's debatable, Abby thought but let it go. She had a lot more she wanted to throw at Robert but she held her tongue. She was in no mood for a debate.

Robert glared at Abby. "Besides, why are you so interested in this?" He gave her a slow suggestive grin. "You aren't jealous are you?"

Disgust welled up in Abby's throat and tasted sour as bile. She chose to ignore his lame question. Robert knew how much she longed for a child and he was doing his best to goad her, no doubt to set her up for a reaction. But he wasn't going to get one. She glanced at Emily who seemed to have missed his little innuendo, thank goodness.

"Abortion is out." Emily said. "I've told you, that's not an option."

Robert shook his head. "Why can't you try to see my side?"

"I'm not going to kill my baby."

"That's ludicrous. You wouldn't be 'killing' anything." Robert made air quotes. He paced back and forth in the foyer, his hands rammed in the back pockets of his Levi's. He weaved around the packages. "What's all this?" He pulled a hand free, gestured toward the bags and looked at Abby. "When did you get so sloppy?"

"We just got back from shopping and haven't had time to put things away." She shot the words at him. "Besides, it's none of your business how I keep house."

Robert threw her a frown and took Emily's arm, guided her toward the living room. "Can we get some privacy around here?"

Just then the doorbell chimed. Abby pulled in a long breath. What now? She opened the door. Sam and Sara stood side by side, expressions grim, and they stared at her.

Sara's face was bright red.

* * *

When Abby opened the door, surprise flicked across her eyes. Her face was flushed.

"Hello, Abby," Sam said. "I need to talk to you."

She stepped back. "Come in."

Sam took his daughter's arm and they stepped across the threshold. He pulled the pack of pills from his pocket and extended it toward Abby. "Want to explain this?"

She glanced at the pills, then shifted her gaze toward his daughter. Sara, silent for a change, stood there and shifted her weight from one foot to the other, her head held low. She made no effort to make eye contact with the nurse.

Abby looked at him. "I don't know what you want me to say."

"I want you to explain what you meant by going behind my back and giving my daughter birth control? Good grief, she's only fourteen." Sam gave her an intent look, and prayed she could say something to clear this up "What were you thinking?"

Abby drew her brows together. "Have you talked to Sara?"

He nodded and looked at his daughter. "We had a lengthy discussion in the car on the way over here."

"You talked. I listened." Sara pulled her arms tight across her chest.

Abby pursed her lips. "I see."

Sam heard voices coming from the other room, voices that did not sound happy. Have we interrupted something?"

Abby pulled in a long breath, held it a couple seconds before she blew it out. Her gaze met Sam's. "It's Emily and Robert."

"Oh."

"Come in the kitchen. I've got coffee made and I'll get Sara a Coke."

Sam could do without the coffee, but he sensed Abby wanted to give her sister, as well as herself, some privacy. He followed her to the kitchen and lowered himself into a chair at the table. Sara looked like a robot, arms by her sides and her hands on her hips. He pulled out a chair and motioned for her to sit. She did. Then predictably she retrieved her cell from her jeans.

"Oh, no you don't," he said. "Turn that thing off."

"Sheesh." Sara rolled her eyes but she turned off the phone and slid it back in her pocket.

His thoughts scrambled with tension as he watched Abby scurry around the kitchen. Whatever anger he felt should be directed at the source, he reminded himself. He shouldn't take it out on Abby.

Abby gathered cups for the coffee. She pulled a Coke from the fridge, filled a tall glass with ice and poured the contents into the glass. Foam rolled over the sides. Abby shook her head, grabbed a rag and wiped the side of the glass, then the counter. She was definitely rattled.

"I'm sorry we just busted in on you," Sam said. "I guess I should have called first."

"Don't worry about it." She looked at him and motioned toward the doorway. "They've got some issues to work through. They don't need me."

Sam felt bad he walked in right in the middle of a crisis. But he was having a crisis too. It wasn't every day he learned the woman he cared about had started his daughter on birth control without so much as a hint to him what was going on.

"I hope he'll get out of here soon." Abby placed cups on a tray beside the glass of Coke, filled them with coffee and carried the tray to the table, set it down. She pulled out a chair and slid into the seat.

Sam raked his fingers through his hair, took a slow breath, and tried to calm down. "Okay, Abby.

Tell me, please. Why did you keep the birth control pills a secret from me? You, of all people, know what I've been going through." He looked at Sara who dropped her head. He turned back and faced the woman who had the power to break his heart. "Why, Abby?"

She morphed into nursing mode. "I'm not at liberty to discuss anything about Sara with you. You know that. You know as well as I do about the legal aspects of being a medical professional." Sincerity flooded her voice but the words stabbed his heart.

"Oh, yeah, Abby. I know all about HIPAA." Sam felt the truth churn in his gut. "But let me tell you something. It's a different story when it's my little girl this happened to."

Sara snorted. "I'm not a little girl."

Abby looked from Sara to Sam and opened her mouth to speak, then closed it when a shriek sounded from the other room.

CHAPTER THIRTEEN

A sudden sharp cry from the other room brought Abby instantly to her feet. She ran into the living room, Sam and Sara on her heels. Robert stood in the middle of the room, eyes wide, mouth gapped open. He pointed to several drops of blood on the floor then hitched his thumb toward the bathroom.

Alarm ran through Abby. She pushed into the bathroom just as Emily stepped into the shower. "What happened?"

"I don't know," Emily said, tears running down her cheeks. "I'm bleeding."

"Are you cramping?"

Emily nodded. "It hurts."

"That's not good. Skip the shower." Abby tossed her a towel. "I'll get you some clean clothes." She bolted to Emily's room, pulled underwear and jeans from her drawer and stepped back in the bathroom.

"Here, put these on," Abby said.

Emily nodded and took the clothes.

Abby folded a hand towel and handed it to her

sister. "Use this for padding," she said and stepped back in the hall.

Three pair of inquisitive eyes looked at her.

"Emily's still bleeding," she said. "I've got to get her to the hospital."

Sam touched her arm. "I'll drive. You're too upset to be behind the wheel."

Abby nodded and headed back to her sister's room and snatched up Emily's purse.

Robert stepped into the room, walked over to Abby and took her arm. "You know," he said, and smiled down at her. "I've never been able to get over you."

"Huh?" What was all his babble about at a time like this?

"I still love you, Abby. I never stopped." He tightened his grip on her arm. "I was crazy for not wanting to marry you. Abs, I want another chance."

Abby jerked her arm free. How could she have ever loved this egotistical man? "Get a grip. Good grief. We've got to get Emily to the hospital."

"Will you give me another chance?" He leaned in close, invaded her space.

Unless Emily's condition totally addled her brain, she swore Robert wanted to kiss her. It certainly unsettled her but she was even more unnerved by his total lack of empathy for her sister's predicament.

She pushed him back. "Stop it, Robert. I never— and let me emphasize the word never, so you can get it perfectly straight—want to have anything more to do with you. I don't know how I could have missed what a jerk you are when we were together.

167

Now back off. Emily is about to lose her baby. Your baby. And she needs you."

"She's already lost the baby." Robert shrugged. "Nothing I can do to help her now." He walked to the door and turned back to Abby. "Don't worry, neither one of you will see me again. Tell Emily I said goodbye."

Abby stared after him as he walked out the door, out of Emily's life. Just as easily as he walked out on her. Only she hadn't been carrying his baby, thank goodness.

With Emily's purse draped over her shoulder, Abby flew back to the bathroom.

"Am I losing the baby?" Tears streamed down her sister's face.

Abby's breath caught in her throat. "I hope not. But we have to get you to the hospital." Abby helped her finish dressing and took her hand as they walked into the living room.

Emily's eyes scanned the room. "Where's Robert?"

"He had to go," Abby said as she led her across the threshold.

"Had to go? Where?"

Abby shrugged. "I don't know."

Fresh tears filled Emily's eyes. "I can't face this alone."

"You're not alone," Abby assured her. "I'm right here."

Sam opened the car door and helped Abby ease Emily into the back seat. Abby ran around the car and scooted in beside her sister. Sam and Sara took the front seat.

Abby slipped an arm around her pregnant sister and noted the drawn, pinched look around her mouth and her lack of color. "Hang in there. We'll get you help soon."

Emily buried her face in Abby's shoulder and cried silently while Abby gently stroked her sister's hair. She was thankful Sam was in the driver's seat. She couldn't have made this trip alone.

Abby glanced at Sara who sat wide-eyed, looking at them from the passenger seat, her eyes pooled with tears.

"Is she okay?" the young girl said, barely above a whisper.

"I hope so," Abby said. "I pray to God she is."

* * *

The ride seemed to take forever, but finally Sam pulled into the emergency entrance. The back doors flew open. Medics hurried to the car. One pushed a wheelchair.

"We've got a possible spontaneous abortion in progress," Sam said.

He opened the back door and stepped aside while the medics gathered Emily and placed her in the chair. The vacated seat was bright red.

His daughter stood by the door, a hand over her mouth, gazing at the dark red stain. "Is she going to die, Dad?" Sara whispered.

Sam put his arm around her shoulder and pulled her close. "No, sweetie." He glanced over his daughter's head at Abby. "She'll be just fine."

The medics rushed Emily through the emergency

entrance. Sam, Abby, and Sara ran after them.

Nurses rushed to meet the wheelchair and exchanged information with the medics as they wheeled Emily across the floor and around a corner. Abby moved alongside the wheelchair, Sam and Sara followed behind.

They reached a room. The nurses pushed the chair behind a curtain. Abby started to follow.

A nurse stepped in front of her and pointed toward the reception area. "You guys need to wait out there."

"I'm her sister. I want to stay with…" Abby started but was interrupted.

"Believe me, there's nothing you can do right now and the doctor will need room to work." The nurse gave her a firm look. "Stay with your friends in the waiting room. We'll come out and give you an update as soon as we can."

The door closed.

Sam guided Abby to the admissions desk in the ED, then settled Sara in a chair in the waiting room. He pulled out his cell phone and hit the button for Florence. She answered on the second ring and he gave her a short version of what was going on.

"Can you come and stay with Sara?" He winked at his daughter and gave her a pat, then turned his head and lowered his voice to just above a whisper. "She's pretty shook, Florence."

"I'm on my way. Be there in five minutes."

Sam slid his cell back in his pocket and looked at Sara. "I'll be right over there with Abby." He pointed to the desk a few feet away. "You okay?"

Sara nodded. But she didn't look okay. He

squatted down beside her and laid his hands on her thighs. "I know it looked like a lot of blood back there. But trust me, Emily's going to be okay."

"Nurse Abby looks so scared."

"She is. That's why I want to stay with her."

She wiped a hand across her eyes. "Go on. Go help Nurse Abby. I'm okay. Really."

Sam stepped to Abby's side and she handed him Emily's purse. "Would you find her medical card?"

He looked through the wallet for her insurance card and handed it to the receptionist while Abby answered what seemed like a blur of non-ending questions.

True to her word, Florence was there in record time. She gave Sam a quick hug, then laid her hand on Abby's shoulder. "I'm so sorry. If there's anything I can do let me know."

A tearful Abby nodded.

Florence looked up at Sam. "Don't worry about Sara, I'll look after her real good. We'll be in the cafeteria."

"Thanks." He watched Florence, never more thankful than right now that he had a friend like her, as she gathered Sara and headed down the hall.

The forms completed, Abby slid her chair back and stood. She looked toward the double doors, her face ashen. Sam reached for her trembling hand, laced her cold fingers with his and guided her to the waiting area. "We've done all we can do. Now it's just a matter of waiting."

"I know." She looked from his face to their hands and he noticed she didn't pull back. In fact she was holding on to him with all her strength.

A few minutes later Florence appeared with two steaming cups of coffee. "I dumped a whole lot of cream into yours, Abby."

Abby gave Florence a weak smile. Only then did she release her grip of Sam's hand. She reached for the coffee and took a sip. "Thank you."

"I thought you guys might need this." Florence handed the other cup to her friend. "And don't you worry about Sara. I got her something to eat and I'm keeping her company," she said as she walked away.

Abby set the cup on the floor beside her chair and pulled out her cell. "I've got to call Mom." She tapped in a series of numbers.

Sam let his thoughts drift as he half listened to Abby's conversation with her mother. He sucked in a sharp breath at the frightful but realistic logic of the situation. Emily was apparently in the process of a miscarriage. All that blood, and if the doctor couldn't get it stopped…

"Thanks for staying with me." Abby interrupted his reflections. "I don't know what I would do if you weren't here."

He nodded. "I wouldn't want to be anywhere else."

"About Sara. Sam, I'm sorry. I wanted to tell you about the pills. I was so torn up…"

"It's okay." He knew she had acted in accordance with her professional ethics. "I understand. And actually, I'm the one who should apologize. I'm not happy Sara's problems have cascaded down on me, but that's not your fault and I should never have blamed you. You were simply doing your job. I'm sorry I questioned that. I was wrong."

Abby looked at him intently. "You know, I'd never hurt you."

"I know." And he did know. Abby didn't have a mean bone in her body.

Eternal minutes ticked by. People came and went in the ED. Finally an hour later, the double doors opened and a man dressed in blue scrubs with brown wavy hair and a craggy face walked toward them. He stopped, his gaze swept over them. "I'm Doctor Stanford. Are you Emily's family?"

Abby jumped up. "I'm her sister."

Sam rose to his feet, muscles tense, and awaited the verdict.

"How is she?" Renewed tension tightened Abby's features. "Is she okay?"

"Yes, she is fine. But we couldn't save the baby. I am so sorry." The doctor held up a hand in a calming gesture. "And due to the excessive bleeding and other complications, I had to do a hysterectomy. She's lost a lot of blood, but she will make a complete recovery."

"Oh, no." Abby's hands flew to her flushed cheeks. "Poor Emmy. Does she know? About the baby? About the surgery?"

"I've told her but she's still pretty groggy. When she's fully awake I'll talk to her again. Explain everything to her."

Sam watched shock turn to worry on Abby's pale face and she said, "You're sure she's okay?"

"I'm positive." The doctor gave Abby a little smile. "You're Abby?"

Abby nodded.

"She's been asking about you. Give the nurses time to move her out of recovery and into a room and then you can see her." He turned and walked back through the double doors.

Tears welled in Abby's eyes. "She'll never be able to have children."

Sam guided her to a chair and he sat beside her. "I hate that for her," Sam said. "She's so young."

She dropped her head into her hands and cried openly, silently. Sam laid a hand on her shoulder and patted her gently to give her time to deal with her grief.

"I can't even imagine how she's going to take this," she said. "She'll be devastated. I know I would be. Both of us have always dreamed of a big family someday." She dug a tissue from her purse and wiped her face and blew her nose.

Sam nodded. "I hear you. Me too."

Abby snuffled. She drew her brows together and gave him a long look. "You too?"

"Yes. I've always wanted a big family."

"But that day at the stables you said you were glad you didn't have any more kids to contend with."

He shook his head. "I must have been frustrated to say something like that. I love kids. I want lots of them."

CHAPTER FOURTEEN

As Abby sat beside Sam in the waiting room, a wave of excitement swept over her. He did want more kids. She smiled and the smile flooded through her and made the pit of her stomach tingle. Then she thought of Emmy, barren in the recovery room, and how Robert abandoned her. The smile faded and a chill raced through her body.

"Cold?" Sam asked. He scooted closer and draped an arm around her.

"Not really. I'm thinking about how this is going to affect Emily."

Sam nodded and gave her shoulder a squeeze. She liked the comfort and strength his commandeering hand provided.

After a few moments of comfortable silence, Sam nudged her. "Is that your parents?" He nodded toward the doorway.

Abby glanced to her right, then slid from her chair and stood. Her parents stepped over the threshold, saw her and hurried over.

"We got here as fast as we could." Her dad pulled her into a hug. "Traffic was terrible."

"Is she okay?" Mom asked, just above a whisper.

Abby turned and looked at her mother. Her face was flushed and splotchy and Abby knew she probably cried most of the trip down here.

"After she lost the baby, they couldn't stop the bleeding," Abby said as gently as she could. "And they had to do a hysterectomy."

The color drained from her mom's face and her eyes filled with tears. Her lips trembled when she spoke. "My poor baby."

"Oh my Lord," her father said. His clenched jaw betrayed his tension and she felt a pang of empathy for him. He was always so protective of his daughters. He shielded them from pain whenever he could. "Have you seen her yet?"

Abby shook her head. "Not yet. She's still in recovery."

"It shouldn't be too much longer," Sam said.

Abby laid her hand on Sam's arm. "Mom, Dad, this is Sam Ford. He drove us to the hospital."

"Sorry we had to meet in such difficult circumstances." Sam extended his hand. "But it is nice to meet you. I've heard a lot about you."

Her dad shook Sam's hand. "I'm Jim. This is Mary. Thanks for looking after our little girl."

Sam nodded. "Glad I could help."

Abby motioned to the black vinyl bucket chairs and her parents plopped down. She scooted her chair so she sat across from them. "Emily was at my apartment when the cramping and bleeding started." She felt her eyes moisten, but blinked them clear.

"Thank goodness she wasn't alone."

"Does she know…" Her mom's voice broke and she looked so fragile.

Abby nodded, wishing she could make her mother's heart knit back together.

Her mom sank back in her chair and inhaled a sharp breath. Abby took her hand and gave it a firm squeeze. "The surgery went well," she said. And then, because she wanted so badly to convince herself, she added, "The doctor said she'll be just fine."

"Yes, she will." Her dad agreed. He put his arm around Mary's shoulder and pulled her toward him. "We'll get her through this, Mother."

Just then a nurse, the same one from before, came through the doorway and walked to Abby. "They transferred your sister from recovery. She's on the second floor, room 225. You can move to that waiting area if you'd like. When they get her situated, you can see her for a few minutes."

"How is she?" Abby asked.

The nurse smiled. "She's wide awake now. And she keeps asking about you. I told her I nearly had to barricade the door to keep you away from her." She patted Abby's arm. "Don't worry, we're taking good care of her."

Abby thanked the nurse, stood and pushed her hair back from her face.

Leaving the ED, Abby walked beside Sam and her parents down the quiet hall and stepped into the elevator that took them to the second floor.

It was just past eight in the evening and the hospital had a drowsy air about it. Patients rested while nurses quietly filled out charts and sorted bedtime medication. The group moved quickly down the corridor and settled into the waiting room.

"I'll let the nurses know we're here," Sam said.

"Thanks." Abby smiled at him. He returned the smile, turned and headed down the hall. She directed her attention to her parents. "I don't know how I would have got Emily here without him."

"I'm glad you had someone with you." Her mother massaged the inside corners of her eyes with her thumb and a forefinger.

"Me too." Abby swallowed hard. "Emily was so scared."

"I can only imagine," her mom said and pulled in air. "Have you and Emily patched up your differences?"

Abby looked at her mom and shook her head.

There was a brief hesitation before her mother spoke. "Emily's impulsive, always has been. Yet one thing I know for sure, she loves you, Abby."

Abby sighed. "I'm trying. I just…" Her thoughts stuck in her throat and she couldn't put into words the emotions that whirled through her head.

Her mom's lips turned down and she fixed Abby with a steady gaze. Her way of showing disapproval.

"You know I love her, Mom," Abby said. "But she betrayed me in the worst possible way and I'm having a problem with that. What she did was wrong."

Her mom nodded. "Of course it was wrong. Otherwise you wouldn't have to forgive her."

"If it was anyone besides Robert…" She shook

her head. "She knew how I felt about him. How hurt I'd be."

"Please, Abby," Mom said. "Don't let anything come between you and your sister. Especially now, she's going to need all the support she can get. Just let it go."

"I'm trying Mom. I really am."

"Robert?" Dad huffed out a breath. "As bad as I hate to bring this up, I think someone should let him know Emily's here. He has a right to know."

"He knows," Abby said.

"Oh?" Dad's gaze darkened, his eyes narrowed. "Where is he, then?"

"I don't know. He left right before we did."

"You mean he knew Emily was losing the baby?" Mom arched her brow. "And just walked out?"

Abby nodded. "Something like that." She inhaled, refusing the memory of Robert's final come-on. She hardened herself because when she thought about his actions it made her skin crawl.

"I'll…" Dad raked his fingers through his hair. "If I could get my hands on him right now, I'd..."

"There, there, Jim. Settle down." Mom laid a hand on his arm. "That won't help anything."

"Maybe not."

"You know it won't."

He looked at his wife. "Someone needs to tell him what a scum he is. I'm sick and tired of him using my girls."

"Mom's right," Abby said. "Forget it. He's out of both of our lives now, for good."

"Yeah?" Dad snorted. "We'll see. He's like a

bad penny, he keeps showing up."

"Not this time," Abby said, then turned when Sam walked around the corner.

Sam tossed Abby a smile. "Emily's ready for visitors now."

Abby sprang from her seat. "Okay, let's go see her." Abby grabbed her mother's hand and took a step.

"You go ahead." Her mom pulled back and shook her head. "We'll wait here. She needs a little time alone with her big sister."

Abby froze. She didn't want to go by herself. After everything that had happened how could she face Emily alone? She looked toward Sam.

He laid his hand gently on her arm and his gaze met hers. "It'll be okay," he whispered. "You can do this."

Abby swallowed a breath. She nodded and headed to room 225. She pushed open the door, stepped in, and walked quietly to her sister's bedside.

Emily turned.

"Hi," Abby said. "You okay?"

"A little weak and a lot hoarse."

"That's normal after having an intubation tube removed."

"If you say so." Emily rubbed her hand over her neck. "I feel like a bus drove down my throat."

Abby picked up a glass filled with water and held the straw to Emily's lips. She raised her head from the pillow, took a long pull, then leaned back. Abby set the glass on the bedside table and eyed her sister. Emily's face was pale but that was to be expected. She'd lost a lot of blood. An IV hung by the side of the bed, and Abby followed the tube down to Emily's arm. The black and blue skin suggested someone had used her arm as a pincushion while they tried to insert the needle. Instinctively Abby checked the IV drip.

"Don't be a nurse." Emily patted the bed. "Just be my sister."

"You got it." She lowered herself onto the edge of the bed so as to not jostle it more than she had to. "You scared the daylights out of me, you know."

Emily tried to smile, but Abby could see it hurt.

She gently brushed the hair from her sister's forehead. "Do you need something for pain?"

Emily shook her head.

"If you're sure…" Abby began.

"I'm sure." Emily shifted her position ever so slightly, discomfort creased her face. "All of this is my fault, you know."

"Your fault?"

"Uh huh, punishment. For what I did with Robert."

Abby shook her head, opened her mouth to speak but Emily held up a hand to silence her.

"You know, I was a virgin when I met Robert," Emily said, a faraway look in her eyes. "I was going to save myself for marriage. That's a big laugh now, huh? I knew better than to get involved in a pre-marital affair. But I did it anyway. Just leaped in headfirst. Like you said, Abby, I never think. Never. Anyway I'm paying for it now. And I'll pay for it the rest of my life."

Abby looked in her sister's tear filled eyes and

saw the remorse. "God loves you, Emily."

"God took this baby away from me and He's not going to give me the chance to ever have another one." She wiped a hand across her face. "He's had it with me. I blew it, big time."

She searched for words. "No, Emmy, that's not how Grace works. God's love is unconditional. It will never end."

Emily shook her head as tears leaked from beneath her eyelids.

"And He longs to forgive you, take you back in His arms and heal your broken heart. But then you must forgive yourself."

"How can I? After all I've done. The people I've hurt…"

"Let it go. Don't hang on to the bad things. Just ask God to forgive you, then forgive yourself and go on with your life."

Emily blinked. "You make it sound easy."

"It is easy. God's plan isn't hard."

"I was supposed to be a Christian…"

"Christian's make mistakes, slip up all the time; but we have God to turn to when we need forgiveness and healing."

Emily nodded. She closed her eyes and Abby sensed she was praying. Abby bowed her head and prayed also. When the silent prayers were finished Abby looked at her sister. "Now take the next step, Emmy. Forgive yourself."

Her sister shrugged. "How can I ever…"

"Just do it."

"Okay, okay," Emily said, the whisper of a smile tugging at her lips. She looked at herself in the mirror over the drawers at the end of the bed. "I forgive you, Emily Dennison, for being such a ditz. For being the biggest mess-up of all time."

Abby laughed, but her laughter turned to sadness when she flashed on her own situation. She'd asked God for forgiveness over a year ago, even accepted His mercy and knew beyond any doubt she was forgiven. But she hadn't taken her own advice, the next step in healing. She hadn't forgiven herself. She'd held on to the anger, bitterness, and self-loathing, feeding it every day. She projected all her frustration on Robert and then Emily.

It's time she took her own advice and forgave herself.

She flashed on the nail-scarred hands she saw the afternoon when Sam held her hand. She knew in an instant what it meant. Only the hands of Jesus could set her free. He paid for all her mistakes two thousand years ago and He patiently waited for her to accept it. She felt a peace flow over her and with it a ton of weight lifted as she shook off all the guilty baggage she'd lugged around for over a year.

She met Emily's gaze and guilt washed over her when she thought of how she pushed her sister away. She leaned in and placed a tender kiss on her sister's forehead. "I love you. I'm sorry I was so mad at you and I'm ashamed how badly I treated you."

Emily blinked back tears. She reached for Abby's hand and gripped so tight it almost hurt. Almost, but Abby didn't care if it brought blood. She was never going to let anything come between her and Emmy again.

After a few minutes of tearful confessions between the sisters, Abby said, "Mom and Dad are in the waiting room. They need to see for themselves that you're okay." She stood. "Then, little sister, you're going to ask for something for that pain. And don't give me any arguments."

"I will." Emily gave her a weak smile. "I love you. Thanks for everything." She pulled a tissue from the nightstand and blew her nose. "Send them in. Then you go ahead and head home. I know you're exhausted."

When Abby stepped into the waiting room, Mom and Dad jumped from their seats. "She's waiting to see you," Abby said. Then she looked at her mom and whispered, "Everything's fine between Emily and me."

"Oh, thank the Lord." A smile turned up the corners of her mother's mouth. She pulled Abby to her and gave her a kiss on the cheek. "I knew you girls could work it out."

Her dad patted her on the back. "Go home and get some rest. We'll be there in a little while."

Abby watched her parents walk away, and thought how blessed she was to have a family like hers.

She glanced at Sam and he gave her a wink. "You holding up okay?"

"I am. And I'm just about ready to go, but let me freshen up a little in the ladies room. That will give you some time alone with Sara."

"Thanks." Sam took a step, then turned back toward Abby, took her hand but didn't say anything. They shared a long look that to Abby said it all.

* * *

Sam stopped outside the cafeteria and looked through the glass panel. It was after nine and the area was almost deserted. Florence stood in the snack section, feeding coins into a vending machine.

Sam pushed through the door and walked toward Sara. She sat alone and sipped tea at a small table overlooking the lamppost lit waterfall in the outside atrium. She turned, and when she saw Sam she jumped up and raced to him. Sam wrapped her in his arms, kissed the top of her head.

Florence stepped up to Sam, concern etched her features. "How's Emily."

"She's going to be just fine." Sam tucked Sara into a chair, pulled out the one beside her and scooted up to the table. "She lost the baby though."

"No complications, I hope."

"She had a hysterectomy, but the doctor says she will make a complete recovery."

Florence shook her head. I'll be praying for her and her family." She handed two candy bars to Sam. "Do you still need me to stay here? I can you know."

"No, thanks, we're going home soon. I can't thank you enough for all you've done."

"Shoot, it was nothing. I'm glad I could help. Plus it gave me time to get acquainted with your daughter." She glanced at Sara, then back to Sam. "I guess I'll see you Monday. If you need anything, don't hesitate to call."

"I won't, and thanks again."

Florence strode across the tile and out the door.

"You okay?" Sam handed one of the candy bars to Sara.

She nodded. "I'm glad Emily's going to be okay. But, no kids? Ever?" A frown tugged at her face. "That's awful."

Sam nodded. "Yeah."

"Where's Nurse Abby?"

"She wanted to freshen up a little before we head home," Sam said. "She's had a rough evening."

Sara's eyes welled with tears. Then she was crying full force and Sam's heart broke. He pulled a napkin from the dispenser on the table and tucked it in her hand. "I'm sorry you had to witness all this tonight."

Sara shook her head and wiped the napkin under her nose. "It's more than that. I've had a lot of time to think and... well I don't care that you made me stay here and not go with Mom. I love you and I want you to love me too."

"Oh, Sara." Sam pulled her to him and gave her a hug. "I do love you very much. Don't ever doubt that." He leaned back, squared his shoulders. "Even though it would have devastated me to let you go with your mother, I would never have stopped you. Your mother didn't give either one of us a choice. She made the decision before she ever talked to me. But don't think for one minute I didn't want you with me."

"I'm glad you wanted me." Sara said, a smile tipping up her lips. "And I'm glad I'm with you. I'm sorry for all the hassle I've given you. I've acted like a brat. But I promise things will be different if you'll give me a second chance."

Sam felt moisture in his eyes. He blinked it away as a lump formed in his throat. He pushed her soft hair from her eyes. "You are my second chance."

"Thanks, Dad." Sara smiled through tear filled eyes.

"Come on," he said and slid his chair back. "Let's find Abby and go home."

* * *

Sunday afternoon Sam and Sara headed to the stables to meet Abby. All three of them agreed on the way home the night before to meet at the stables after Abby checked on her sister.

Sam cross tied three horses in the center aisle, saddled them and had them ready to go. He glanced over the back of the big bluish gray mare and saw Abby walking toward them. When she saw him, she smiled, a smile that didn't hold back, that didn't have shadows. "Hey, sunshine."

"Hi, yourself." Abby lowered her sunglasses and strolled toward him. She wore a yellow T-shirt and jeans, and looked like she was ready for a summer outing. To see her was like peace that touched his soul, like hope dawning, all his dreams coming to life.

"You look like you're ready to hit the trail."

"I am." Abby glanced at his daughter and gave her a warm smile. "Hey, Sara. Have you ridden before?"

"Uh huh. I took lessons last year."

Abby raised a brow. "You're an old pro, then."

"Yeah, right." Sara rolled her eyes. "I haven't been back on a horse since the lessons."

"I told her it's like riding a bike," Sam said. "It all comes back to you."

"Your dad knows his stuff about horses, that's for sure." Abby shot him a smile and walked to Hero. The gelding lifted his head, nickered in greeting, glad to see Abby. The big animal turned to putty as he lowered his nose for Abby's affectionate touch. "Hey, Hero. I missed you, you know that?" Abby cooed as she rubbed his muzzle.

Sam shook his head. That animal was sure taken with Abby. "I saddled Cocoa for Sara," he said. "He's the one she learned to ride with."

His daughter walked to her horse's side and glanced at Abby. "I think he remembers me." Cocoa turned his head and Sara stroked his nose, then leaned in and gave it a kiss.

"I'm sure he does," Abby said. "Animals are smart."

One side of Sara's mouth hitched up as she studied her ride. "Hope he's smart enough to let me stay on his back." She directed her next remark directly to Cocoa as she patted his head. "Hear that, boy. You let me stay upright in that saddle, okay?"

Abby smiled then mounted Hero. Sam liked the way she sat so easily, nonchalant, shoulders comfortably squared as if she were born to be on the back of a horse. He drank in her gentleness as she leaned forward and rubbed Hero's neck.

"Uh, Dad... Hello." Sara pulled him back to the moment. He turned toward his daughter who was giving him a question mark gaze. He winked at his beautiful child, then gave her a boost into Cocoa's saddle.

He walked around Savannah and took hold of the saddle horn, threw a leg up and over and then adjusted his weight in the soft leather. "You girls ready?"

They both nodded as they reined their animals toward the path.

As he rode beside Abby and Sara, Sam's heart swelled with emotion. Everything had a different look this afternoon. The trees looked greener, and not just from the rain last night. The birds sang back and forth and sounded distinct, as if they took for granted Sam knew what they talked about. They were in love, rejoicing in the Lord, thanking Him that they were blessed with a perfect mate.

Sam looked from Abby to Sara. They gave him wide grins. He returned their smiles and pulled in a long breath. Thank you, God. Thank you for making my life so perfect, he said under his breath. Then out loud he said, "Are you guys as happy as I am?"

They shot him a look and Abby said, "If you only knew."

CHAPTER FIFTEEN

Monday morning as Abby sat at her desk, a wide yawn stretched her mouth. She suffocated it with the back of her hand, stood, and arched her back. She needed to shake off this draggy brain fog, her day had only started.

A cup of coffee was calling her name so she padded down the hall to the cafeteria and filled the largest mug she could find, and doused it with cream until it looked almost white.

"Looks like we had the same idea," Florence said. Abby turned and looked into the cheerful face of the cook who had her hands wrapped around a steaming cup. "Can you sit and visit with me a minute?"

"Sure." Abby looked at her watch. "I've got a few minutes before my first student.

Abby and Florence plopped down at the nearest table. Florence looked as tired as Abby felt. "Looks like you had a rough night too," Abby said. She tipped the cup and took a small drink of the very warm liquid, letting it slide down her throat.

"Oh, I guess I slept as good as I usually do. When you get older, you don't sleep that well." Florence wiped a hand across her brow. "I'm getting too old to work full time."

"How long have you been here?"

The cook sighed. "Over twenty years."

"Have you thought about retiring?"

"Naw. Can't afford to. A Social Security check wouldn't pay my bills. I'd have to move in with one of my kids and I don't want to interfere with their lives. I guess I'll just plug along here until they kick me out or I fall over dead. Whichever comes first."

Florence's words sounded bleak but the tone was lighthearted. Abby figured the cook would be lost without her job where she could fuss over, and mother everyone.

"So what kept you up last night?" Florence traced her finger around the rim of her cup.

Abby shrugged. "Just one of those nights. My head too full of thoughts, I guess."

"Your sister...?" Florence pulled her brows together, worry creased her face. "Is she doing okay?"

Abby nodded. "She's doing great. In fact she will be discharged from the hospital today. She's going home, back to Mom's." She gave the cook a smile. "Thanks for coming to the hospital Saturday to stay with Sara. I know Sam appreciated it."

"I'd do anything for that man. He's pretty special. I hope you realize that."

"Oh, I do." Abby smiled. "There's no one like Sam."

"I'd hate to see him get hurt." Florence cocked her head to the side and gave Abby a once over. "But you know what? I think I've misjudged you. I think Sam's right. You're pretty special yourself."

Heat rushed up Abby's neck. "Sam said that?"

"It's not always what Sam says. It's what he means."

"Yeah?" Abby laughed. "I bet he can't put anything past you."

"I'd like to see him try." Florence scooted her chair back. "Are there any plans between the two of you I should know about? Do I need to be looking for a special dress…"

Abby laughed. "No, Florence, but rest assured, if there's ever any news, I'm sure you'll be one of the first ones to know."

"I'd hope." Florence gave her a wink. "You know, I'm getting used to you. I'd hate to lose you around here. And I know Sam feels the same way."

"Neither one of you need to worry about losing me."

"Good. Well, I've got to get back to my business."

Florence popped up from her chair and Abby noticed she didn't hesitate or stumble. No more vertigo, her meds did the trick. That made Abby smile.

"See you later," Abby said. She picked up her cup and headed back to her office.

Ten minutes later, Sara and Brenda strolled into Abby's workspace and slid into chairs across from her.

"Can I get another pregnancy test?" Brenda

dropped her head, her ears pink.

Abby pulled in a calming breath, trying to keep her persona neutral. "Sure." Abby motioned to the bathroom. "Get me a specimen."

When Brenda closed the bathroom door, Abby looked at Sara. "Are you sore from all the riding yesterday?"

Sara shook her head. "Not bad." She rubbed the top of her legs and chuckled. "My quads never knew what hit them though."

"I can relate to that. You should have seen me the morning after my first lesson." Abby wrinkled her nose as she remembered. "I was a mess."

Sara gave her a knowing grin. She shifted positions. "Thanks for keeping your word…you know, not telling my dad about the pills and all."

Abby nodded and smiled. "A promise is a promise."

Sara opened her purse, dug around and pulled out her birth control pills. "Here. I don't need these. I've never…well you know…" She shoved the pills across the desk. "Trust me I don't need these."

Abby picked up the pills, rotated them in her hands. The pack was full. Sara hadn't even started them. "I'm really glad to hear that, Sara. You're a smart young lady and I'm proud of you."

Sara's face brightened and she shook her head. "I don't even have a boyfriend."

"You have plenty of time for boyfriends. And you know what? You'll have lots of them before you meet the right one."

"You think?"

"I know." Abby gave her a long look. "You

don't have to be intimate with a guy for him to care about you."

"Brenda say's you do. She says guys aren't going to hang around if you don't... well, you know."

"Brenda's wrong. I hope, for her sake, she realizes it before she finds herself in a mess she can't get out of." Abby held up the pack of pills. "This is not the answer to meaningful relationships."

"Yeah," Sara said and a soft laugh whispered at her lips. "Asking for the pills was a guise. I guess I was trying to make a point or something. I tried to prove I could be like everyone else." She shrugged and blew out a breath. "I never intended to use them in the first place. Pretty stupid thing to do, huh?"

"Maybe. But what you're doing now is pretty smart, if you ask me."

"You know, you're not so bad. For a nurse you're pretty cool. I kinda like the idea of you and my dad hanging out."

"Thanks." Abby laughed. "You know, I kinda like that idea too."

Brenda sauntered back into the room, flipped her hair over her shoulder and slipped into a chair. "I got it." She gestured toward the bathroom.

Abby gave her a nod, stepped away from her desk and checked the specimen. No HCG— Brenda wasn't pregnant. Relieved, she dumped the cup, peeled off her gloves and washed her hands, then returned to her desk.

She settled in her swivel chair and looked across the desk at Brenda. "Do you want Sara to step out now?"

"No. I tell her everything anyway." Brenda squirmed in the seat, looking uncomfortable. "So what did the test say? Am I pregnant this time?"

"No. It was negative." Abby sighed. "So tell me, what's the problem? Are you not taking the pill like you should?"

"I forget sometimes. Well, a lot of the time."

"Have you thought about the shot? Depo? You wouldn't have to remember to take a pill every day."

Brenda tossed a glance at Sara, then directed her gaze to Abby. "Maybe I don't need anything at all. Sara's been lecturing me for weeks." She giggled and swatted Sara on the arm. "Maybe she's got the right idea about this."

"We're just fourteen…" Sara caught herself and chuckled. "Well, almost fifteen. Why do something that we'll regret down the line?"

"You know," Abby said, smiling at Brenda. "You could take a time out, sort all this out before you make anymore… let's say intimate decisions."

Brenda shrugged. "I'll think about it." She pushed her chair back and stood. "Gotta go now. See you later, Sara. Softball practice this afternoon, remember?"

"I won't forget." Sara slipped from her seat but lingered as her friend walked out the door. "I know my dad worries about me hanging around with Brenda and Melissa. But they aren't half as tough as they act. They're really pretty cool."

"Just be careful that you don't compromise your morals."

"Well…I did do something that Sam would die if he ever found out."

"Oh?" Abby pulled in a sharp breath, waited for Sara to elaborate.

Sara shrugged. "I tried smoking."

"Uh oh. That's sure not cool."

"It was disgusting. Believe me, I'm not doing that again. Brenda and Melissa said they are going to quit." She shook her head. "I hope so. The smell of smoke is repulsive."

Abby smiled. "You know, Sara, I bet your dad wouldn't be so shocked if you shared this with him. He'd be very pleased you feel comfortable enough to confide in him." Abby remembered Sam's concern over the smoke he'd smelled on Sara's clothes. This confession would put his mind at ease, show him his daughter could make wise choices after all.

"I think I will." Sara raised her brow. "No more secrets. That'll just get you into trouble." She turned and walked to the door. "Thanks for everything," she shot over her shoulder, then disappeared down the hall.

Relief washed over Abby. Sara was okay. And Sara and Sam were going to be just fine too. He had a daughter that had a lot going for her.

She looked at her watch. Three more hours until she'd meet Sam for lunch. How could she hold out for another one-hundred-eighty minutes without a dose of that man? When she swallowed past the sudden longing that tightened her throat, she knew she was destined to love again. She laughed out loud as she opened her drawer and pulled out a folder.

* * *

Sam pulled the golf cart to the curb just as Abby stepped through the front door.

"Perfect timing," he said as Abby slipped in beside him, smelling like fresh apricots and looking a lot like Greta Garbo looked in her prime.

"Great minds think alike they say." Abby tossed her hair back and gave him a smile that lit up her entire face.

"What's got you in such a good mood?" he asked.

"Professional secrets. But all good, Sam. All good." She patted his arm. "Nothing that makes me feel one bit bad about keeping confidentiality this time."

Sam gave her a sideway glance and felt his heartbeat kick up a notch. He just sat there tapping his fingers on the steering wheel, lost in the moment.

Abby laughed. "Are we going to sit here all day, or are we going to eat?"

"Eat." Sam shifted the cart into gear and pulled it into the street. "Let me guess. You're starved, right?"

"You know me too well."

He tossed her a wink and couldn't stifle a slow grin. "Not well enough. But I'm determined to correct that."

"You're in a pretty good mood today yourself." She angled her head toward him. "I like seeing you this way."

"I like seeing you any way." The huskiness in his voice surprised him and he felt heat rush up his neck. He tried to shake off his embarrassment, concentrate on driving. With Abby close to his side it was hard to think about anything except her. He found it harder and harder to imagine life without her. He knew he'd not emerge unscathed if he let her walk away.

He turned the cart onto the narrow path and wound through the fragrant vegetation on the trail that led to the shoreline. He stopped in front on an ancient and gnarled oak tree. The lake, their special place, loomed in the near distance. He pulled in air, the pungent smell of orange blossoms wafted over him. He reached in the back and pulled out a cooler.

Abby's brows shot up. "Not just sandwiches today?"

He shook his head. "No. I brought leftover shrimp and macaroni salad. Sara and I had a feast yesterday."

"Yum." Abby shot him a look and glided the tip of her tongue over her lower lip. All the encouragement he needed to know she appreciated the extra steps he took this morning. He liked to do things that pleased her. He liked it a lot.

In silence they stepped quickly through the dense foliage and covered the few steps to the bench overlooking the lake.

They laughed and talked throughout lunch. Abby shared Emily's progress with him, mentioning her sister would be going home with her mother today. He knew, though the sisters had made peace, Abby was happy to have her apartment back to herself. And Emily would have a doting mother to nurse her back to health.

The remains of their picnic tidied up, Sam turned on the bench, his face only inches from hers. He was taken aback by her beauty as his gaze caught hers. A man could drown in those emerald pools she called eyes. His focus dropped to her lips, then rose again to her eyes.

"Abby. I…" A tremor ran through his words, caused as much by her closeness as nerves. And what he wanted to say died on his tongue.

His breath caught in his throat. He extended his hand, gently ran his fingers through her silky hair. His heart pounded in his chest so hard he wondered if Abby could hear it. He tilted his head, leaned in and gently brushed his lips across her soft, full lips. The contact was gentle, caressing. Yet the impact of it reverberated through every nerve in his body, and left him feeling as unsteady as a newborn colt. He'd shared many kisses with women in his past but the unexpected potency of this one jolted him.

Shaken, he pulled back a few inches and pinned her with an intent look. Abby's lips parted slightly and the sudden banked fire in her eyes caused his breath to rush from his lungs.

She smiled and leaned in for another kiss.

As Sam tasted her sweetness, Abby's lips stirred beneath his, responding with an eagerness and abandon that made his soul flood with delight. He deepened the kiss, cupping her head with one hand, his fingers tangled in her soft hair.

His heart soared. He knew, beyond any doubt,

this was the woman he wanted to spend the rest of his life with.

EPILOGUE

The wedding was perfect and Abby had never been happier. Her bridesmaids—Emily and Carrie, Sara and Florence looked elegant in their tea length, light purple bridesmaids' dresses when they stood beside her at the altar. They were beautiful, inside and out.

Abby scanned the small reception hall. She spotted her handsome husband in the far corner with Florence, their heads together. No doubt the lovable cook was giving him some last minute advice. Florence tugged on the top of her dress and Abby had to stifle a laugh. The dress had a scooping neckline, and though modest, Abby feared Florence would think it was a bit too much for her. Yet, that was not the case. She oohed and ahhed when she tried it on and admired her reflection in the mirror.

Abby couldn't believe it had been a year since she met Sam. If she had only listened to her heart the first day she saw him, she would have known he was the one for her. But she was filled with so much regret and shame she couldn't trust herself or God.

However, that was all behind her. She allowed herself to shed the last of her fear and open up to Sam, let him into her heart where he belonged.

She turned and watched Sara and Carrie fill plates at the seafood buffet. Sara tossed her hair back and laughed at something Carrie said. They became fast friends over the past year, riding together at the stables whenever Carrie could finagle the time between classes and homework, which was often. Her sister retained the material she studied the first time, unlike Abby who had to make notes of her notes when she was in college.

Sam and his daughter were tight now. All the confusion about her paternity put to rest for good. Sam was such a good dad, but there wasn't much about Sam that wasn't good. She smiled.

"Whenever you're ready, I'll help you change." Emily touched her arm, brought her back to the moment.

"In a while." Abby sighed. "I want to savor every minute of this day."

"I don't blame you," Emily said. "This only happens once in a lifetime."

Abby looked at her sister. Even after all these months, her sister's eyes still held a twinge of sadness that no amount of pretending could mask.

Emily hadn't heard from Robert since the day she lost their baby. It was as if he dropped off the planet. But it wasn't Robert that caused the pain Abby saw in her eyes, she told her. It was the ache in the empty place that had held her womb that reminded her every day that she'd never be able to experience childbirth.

"I'm happy for you, Abs," Emily said. She gave her hand a squeeze. "All your dreams have come true."

Abby nodded. "They have, haven't they?" Abby laid her other hand on top of Emily's. Her sister had gone through a lot but she was healing and Abby knew in time she'd find peace and happiness. Just like I have, she thought. "Your day is coming too, Em."

Silence greeted her comment and a flash of regret tightened Emily's features for a brief beat. "My life is good," she said. "I love my new job. Changing careers has opened up a whole new chapter for me, helped me get my head on straight."

"You're a trooper; I'll have to give you that. My sister, the workaholic. Who would have thought?"

"What are you guys talking about?" Carrie bounced up to her two older sisters. "I'm not missing anything, am I?"

"Not a thing," Emily said.

"You know, I think it's time to change so Sam and I can head out. I hear Jamaica calling my name."

Carrie sighed and pulled her arms across her chest. She swayed back and forth. "That's where I'm going on my honeymoon."

"You have to find a guy you're willing to commit to first." Emily tossed her baby sister a crooked smile.

Carrie rolled her eyes. "Minor detail. I'll work on it." She directed her gaze to Abby. "Take lots of pictures, especially of Dunn's River Falls. That place has to be the best."

"I will," Abby assured her. She wanted to capture as many memories as she could.

She glanced across the room and locked eyes with Sam. He held her gaze as he took a step forward and headed her way. She knew she would make new memories every day with the wonderful man that walked toward her, his mouth turned up at the corners as he gave her a meaningful wink.

Warmth flooded through her. She'd been given a second chance. It was now— and for the rest of her life.

ABOUT THE AUTHOR

Lois Curran was born in Arkansas, raised in Salem, Oregon and moved to Missouri when she was fifteen.

She holds a position as Director of Nursing at the Laclede County Health Department. She has been a nurse for many years and brings her love of healing and years of experience into the character of Abby, the female protagonist in her debut novel, Destined to Love Again.

Writing has always been a passion, but she never made the time. However she'd talked about it for years. Then one day her son Lon gave her some books on how to write a novel. He told her 'Mom it's time to write your book', and she did.

Curran is a member of Ozarks Romance Authors, American Christian Fiction Writers and Sleuths' Ink Mystery Writers.